nickelode

SANJAY & CRAIG™

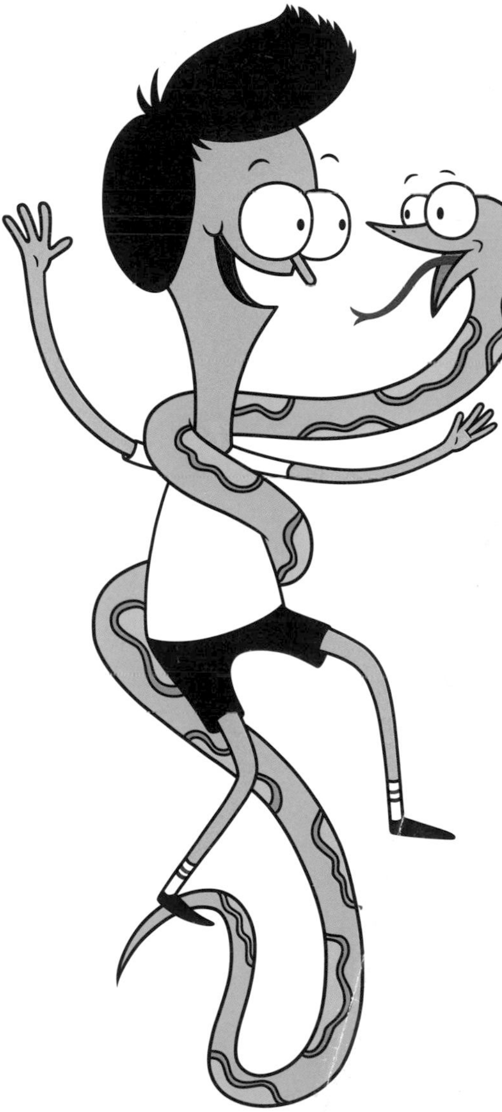

PAPERCUTZ™
New York

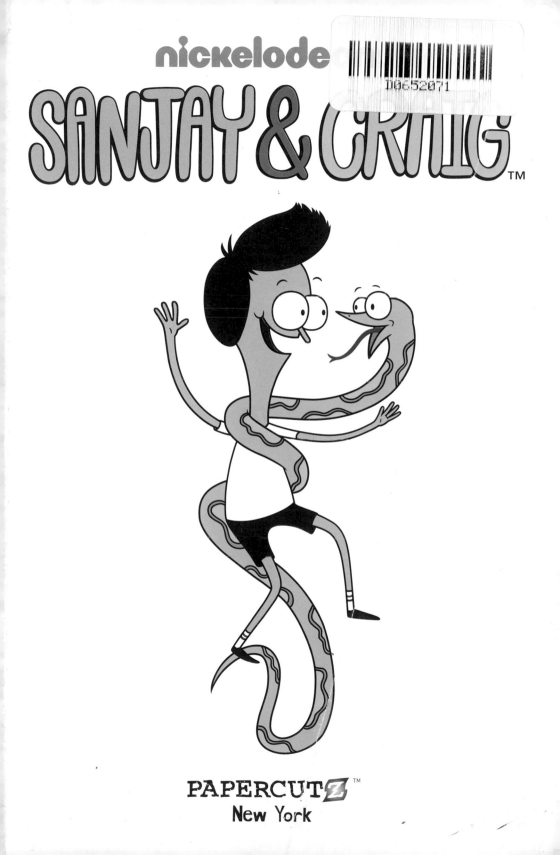

nickelodeon GRAPHIC NOVELS AVAILABLE FROM PAPERCUTZ

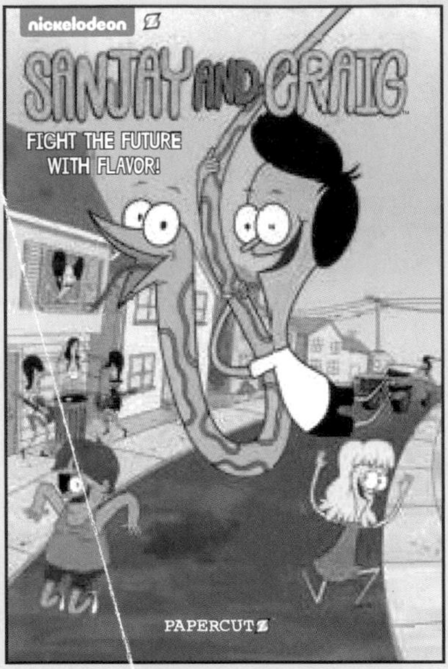
nickelodeon
SANJAY AND CRAIG
FIGHT THE FUTURE WITH FLAVOR!
PAPERCUTZ

#1 "Fight the Future with Flavor"

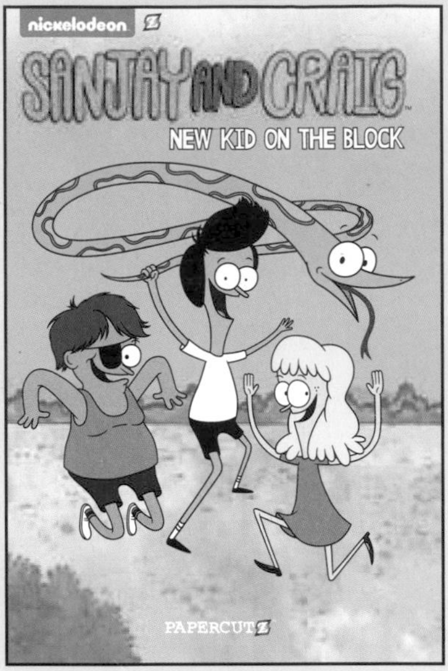
nickelodeon
SANJAY AND CRAIG
NEW KID ON THE BLOCK
PAPERCUTZ

#2 "New Kid on the Block"
COMING SOON!

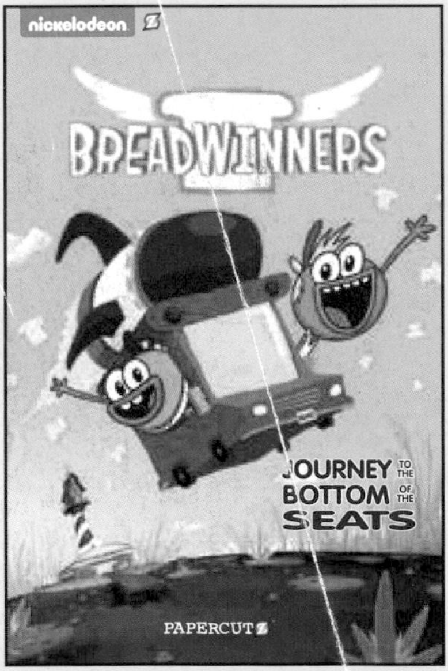
nickelodeon
BREADWINNERS
JOURNEY TO THE BOTTOM OF THE SEATS
PAPERCUTZ

#1 "Journey to the Bottom of the Seats"
COMING SOON!

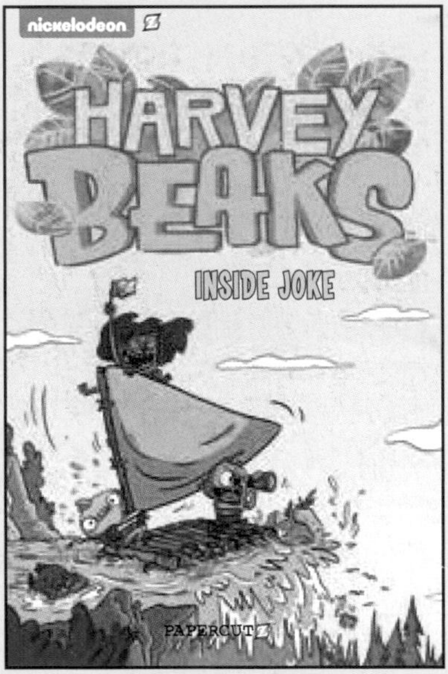
nickelodeon
HARVEY BEAKS
INSIDE JOKE
PAPERCUTZ

#1 "Inside Joke"
COMING SOON!

Nickelodeon graphic novels are available for $7.99 in paperback, $12.99 in hardcover.
Available from booksellers everywhere. You can also order online from Papercutz.com.
Or call 1-800-886-1223, Monday through Friday, 9-5 EST. MC, Visa, and AmEx accepted.
To order by mail, please add $4.00 for postage and handling for first book ordered,
$1.00 for each additional book and make check payable to NBM Publishing.
Send to: Papercutz, 160 Broadway, Suite 700, East Wing, New York, NY 10038.

Nickelodeon graphic novels are also available digitally wherever e-books are sold.

DUDE!

nickelodeon

SANJAY AND CRAIG™

TABLE OF CONTENTS

SANJAY AND CRAIG™

#1 "FIGHT THE FUTURE WITH FLAVOR"

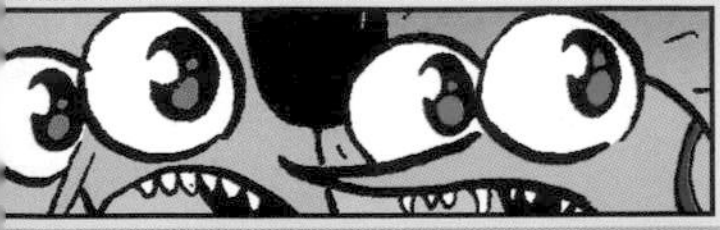

"FIGHT THE FUTURE WITH FLAVOR"
Eric Esquivel – Writer
Sam Spina – Artist & Letterer
Laurie E. Smith – Colorist

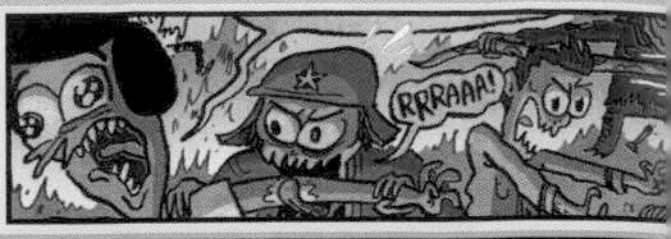

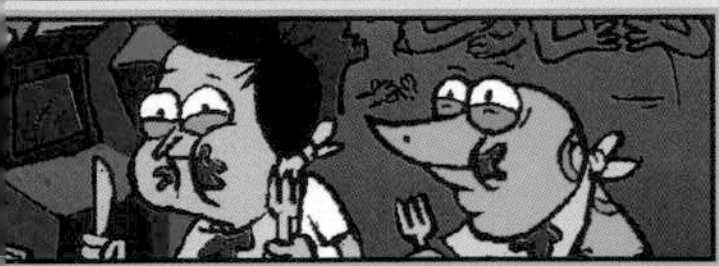

"HOT WINGS FROM HECK"
Eric Esquivel – Writer
James Kaminski – Artist
Laurie E. Smith – Colorist
Tom Orzechowski – Letterer

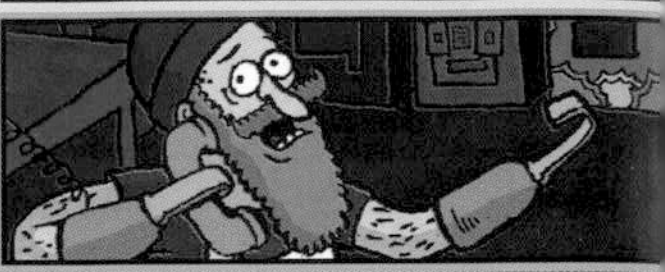

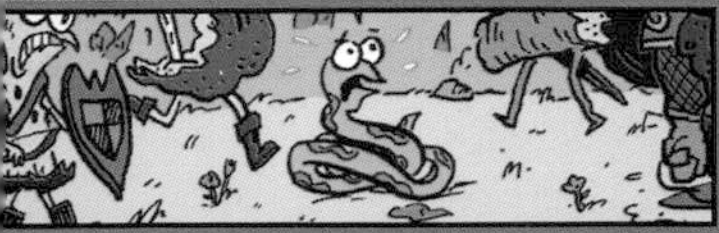

"LORD OF THE PIPES"
Eric Esquivel – Writer
Sam Spina – Artist & Letterer
Laurie E. Smith – Colorist

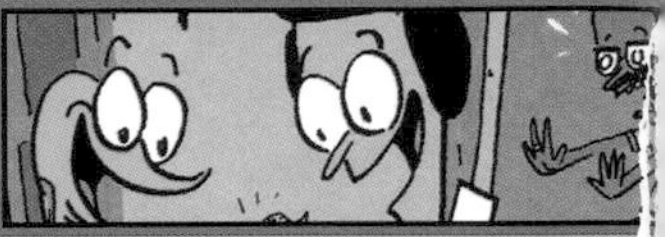

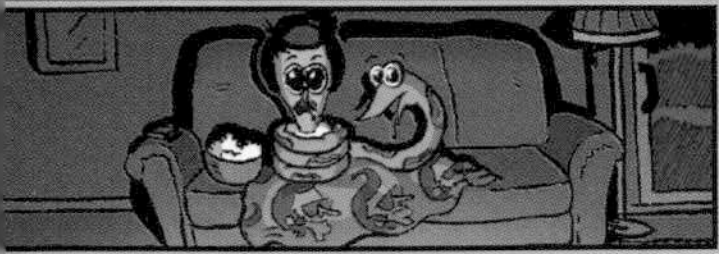

"ALIEN BUTTOPSY"
Eric Esquivel – Writer
James Kaminski – Artist
Laurie E. Smith – Colorist
Tom Orzechowski – Letterer

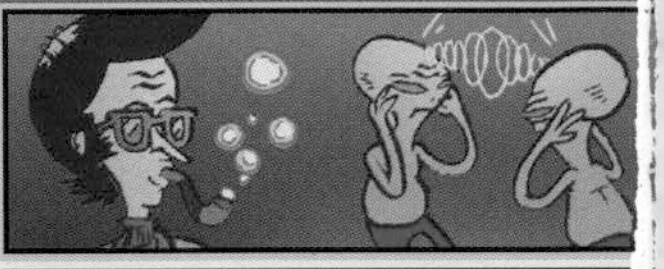

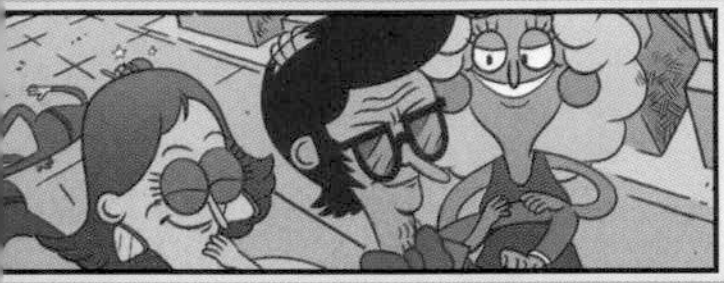

"THE BUTTERMILK KING"
Eric Esquivel – Writer
Ryan Jampole – Artist
Laurie E. Smith – Colorist
Tom Orzechowski – Letterer

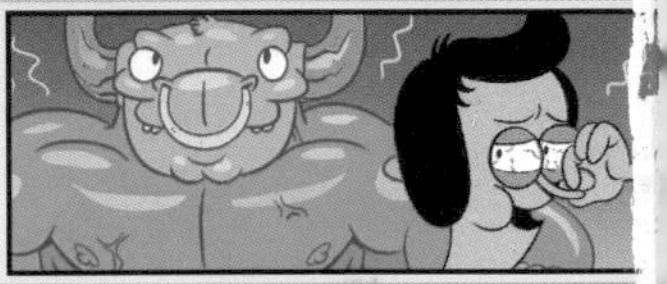

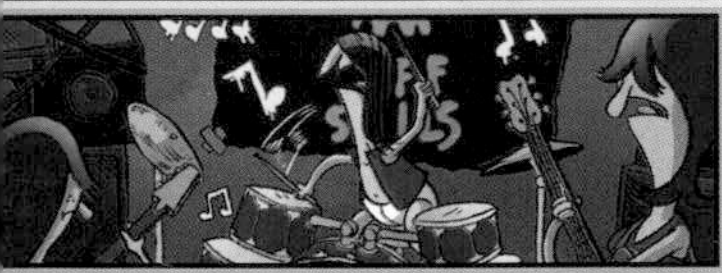

"RATED 'R' FOR RADICAL"
Eric Esquivel – Writer
James Kaminski – Artist
Laurie E. Smith – Colorist
Tom Orzechowski – Letterer

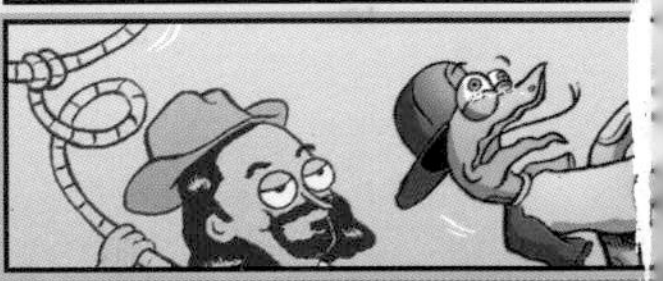

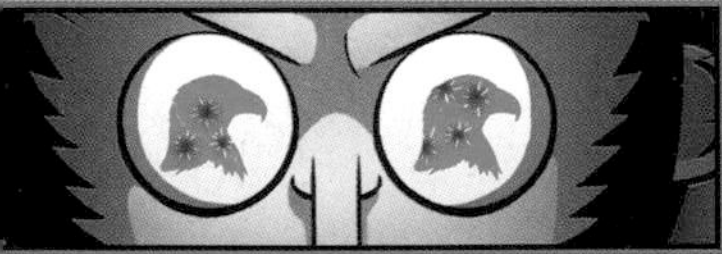

TUFFLIPS MOVIE TRAILERS
Eric Esquivel – Writer
Ryan Jampole – Artist
Laurie E. Smith – Colorist
Tom Orzechowski – Letterer

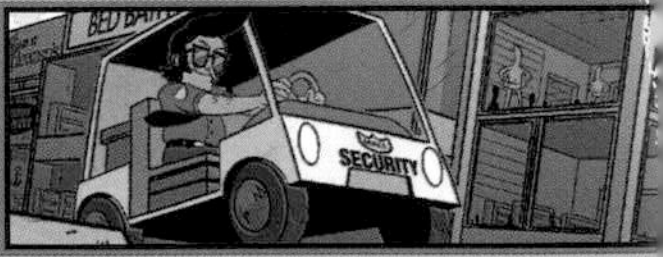
SECURITY

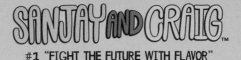

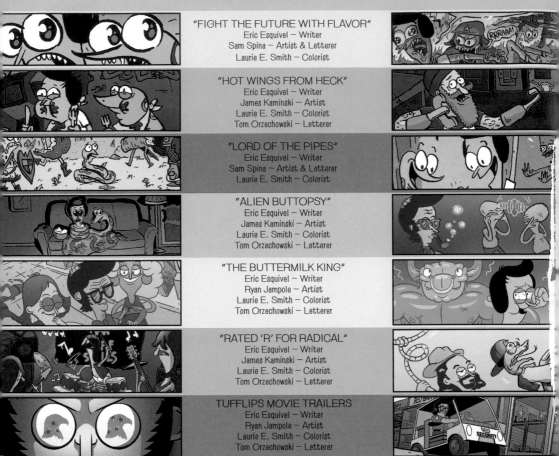

James Salerno – Sr. Art Director/Nickelodeon
Chris Nelson – Design/Production
Jeff Whitman – Production Coordinator
Bethany Bryan, Suzannah Rowntree, Michael Petranek – Editors
Joan Hilty – Comics Editor/Nickelodeon
Dan Berlin, Dani Breckenridge – Editorial Interns
Jim Salicrup
Editor-in-Chief

ISBN: 978-1-62991-302-5 paperback edition
ISBN: 978-1-62991-303-2 hardcover edition

Printed in Canada
September 2015 by Friesens Printing
1 Printer Way
Altona, MB R0G 0B0

FSC www.fsc.org MIX Paper from responsible sources FSC® C016245

Distributed by Macmillan

First Printing

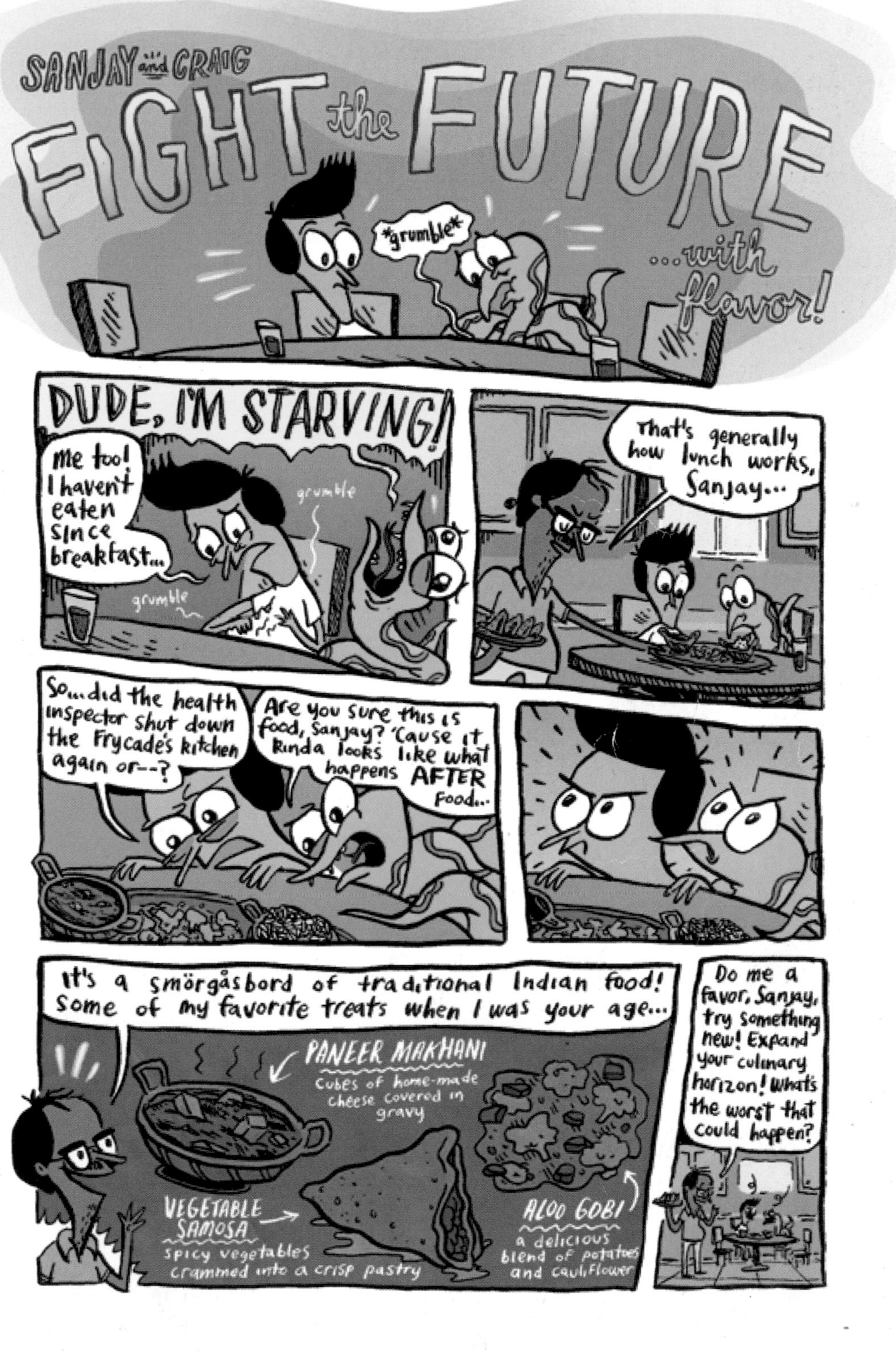
SANJAY and CRAIG
FIGHT the FUTURE
...with flavor!
grumble
DUDE, I'M STARVING!
Me too! I haven't eaten since breakfast...
grumble
grumble
That's generally how lunch works, Sanjay...
So... did the health inspector shut down the Frycade's kitchen again or--?
Are you sure this is food, Sanjay? 'Cause it kinda looks like what happens AFTER food...
It's a smörgåsbord of traditional Indian food! Some of my favorite treats when I was your age...
PANEER MAKHANI
Cubes of home-made cheese covered in gravy
VEGETABLE SAMOSA
spicy vegetables crammed into a crisp pastry
ALOO GOBI
a delicious blend of potatoes and cauliflower
Do me a favor, Sanjay, try something new! Expand your culinary horizon! What's the worst that could happen?

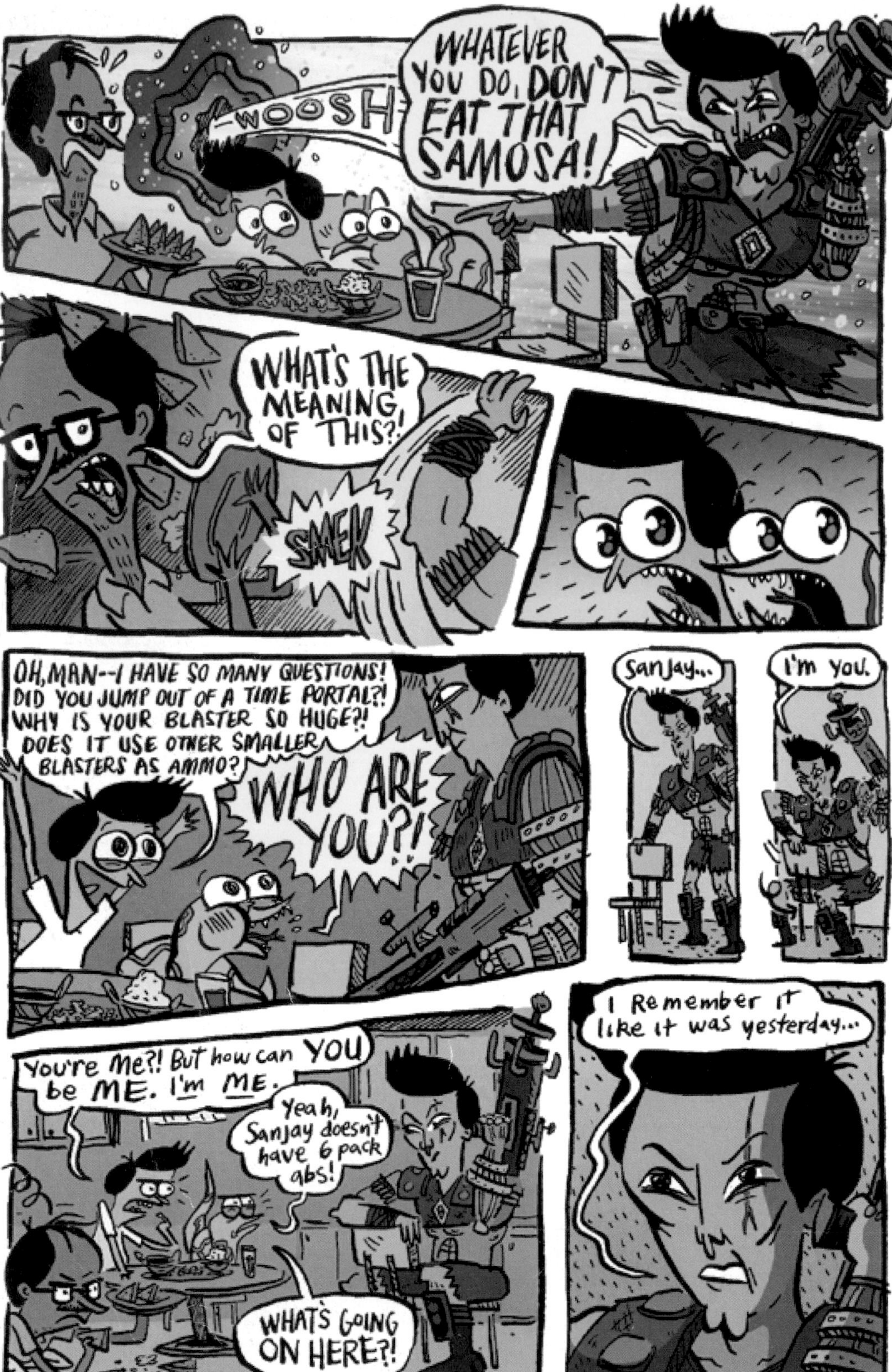
WOOSH
WHATEVER YOU DO, DON'T EAT THAT SAMOSA!
WHAT'S THE MEANING OF THIS?!
SMEK
OH, MAN--I HAVE SO MANY QUESTIONS! DID YOU JUMP OUT OF A TIME PORTAL?! WHY IS YOUR BLASTER SO HUGE?! DOES IT USE OTHER SMALLER BLASTERS AS AMMO?
WHO ARE YOU?!
Sanjay...
I'm you.
You're me?! But how can YOU be ME. I'm ME.
Yeah, Sanjay doesn't have 6 pack abs!
WHAT'S GOING ON HERE?!
I Remember it like it was yesterday...

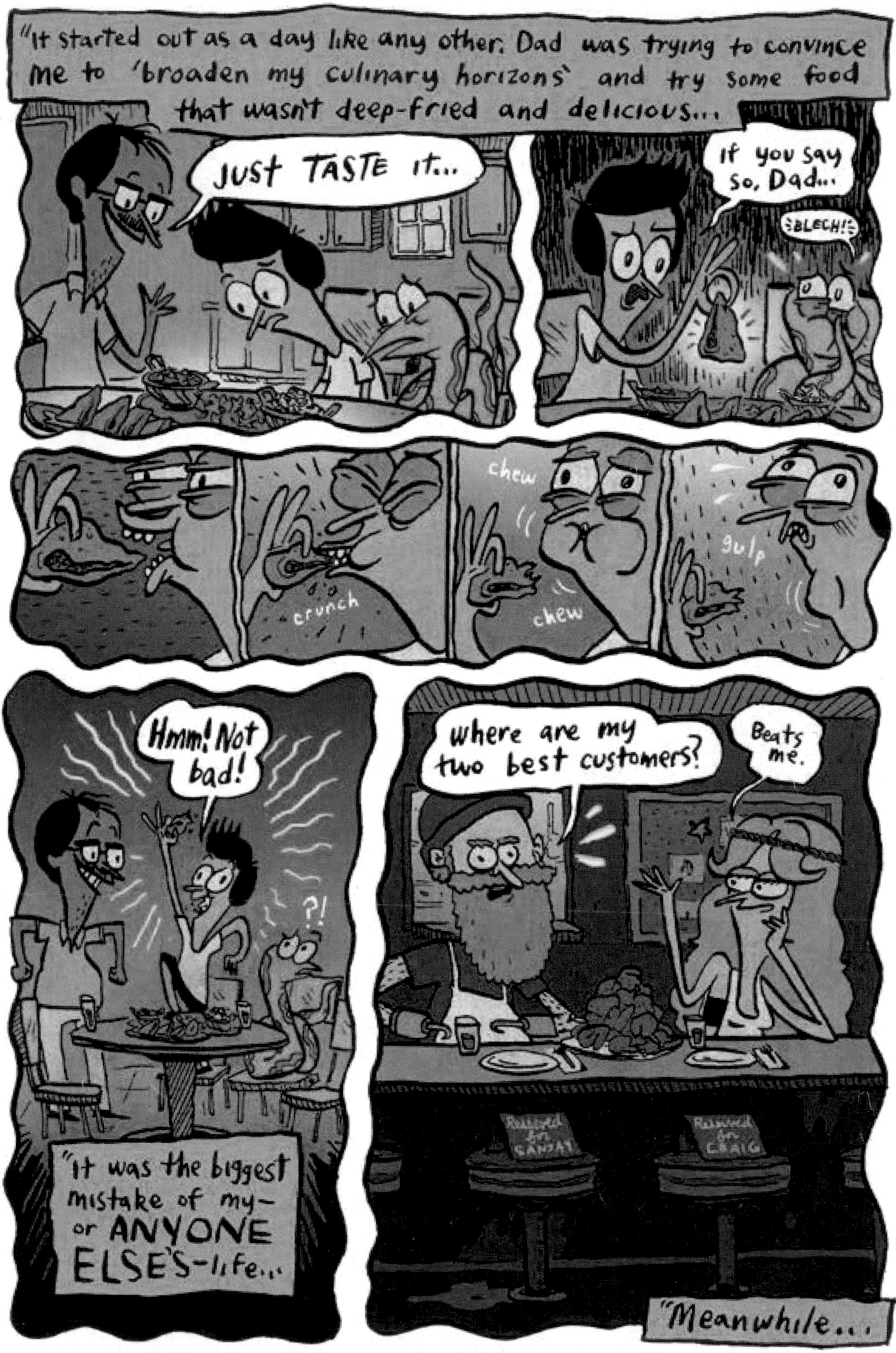

"It started out as a day like any other. Dad was trying to convince me to 'broaden my culinary horizons' and try some food that wasn't deep-fried and delicious...
JUST TASTE it...
If you say so, Dad...
BLECH!
crunch
chew
chew
gulp
Hmm! Not bad!
?!
"It was the biggest mistake of my— or ANYONE ELSE'S—life...
Where are my two best customers?
Beats me.
"Meanwhile...

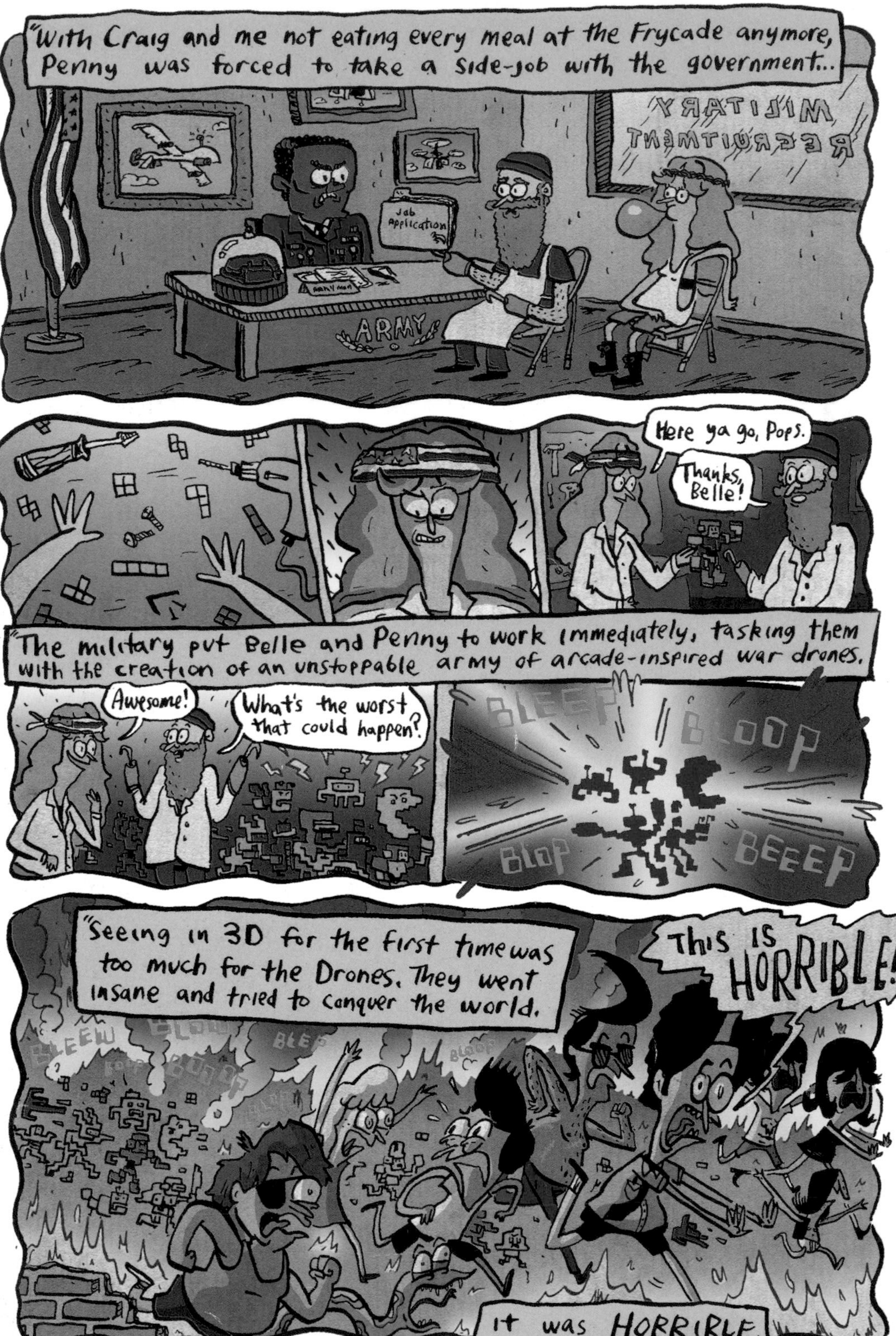
"With Craig and me not eating every meal at the Frycade anymore, Penny was forced to take a side-job with the government...
MILITARY RECRUITMENT
Job Application
ARMY
Here ya go, Pops.
Thanks, Belle!
"The military put Belle and Penny to work immediately, tasking them with the creation of an unstoppable army of arcade-inspired war drones.
Awesome!
What's the worst that could happen?
BLEEP
BLOOP
BLOP
BEEEP
"Seeing in 3D for the first time was too much for the Drones. They went insane and tried to conquer the world.
This IS HORRIBLE!
It was HORRIBLE.

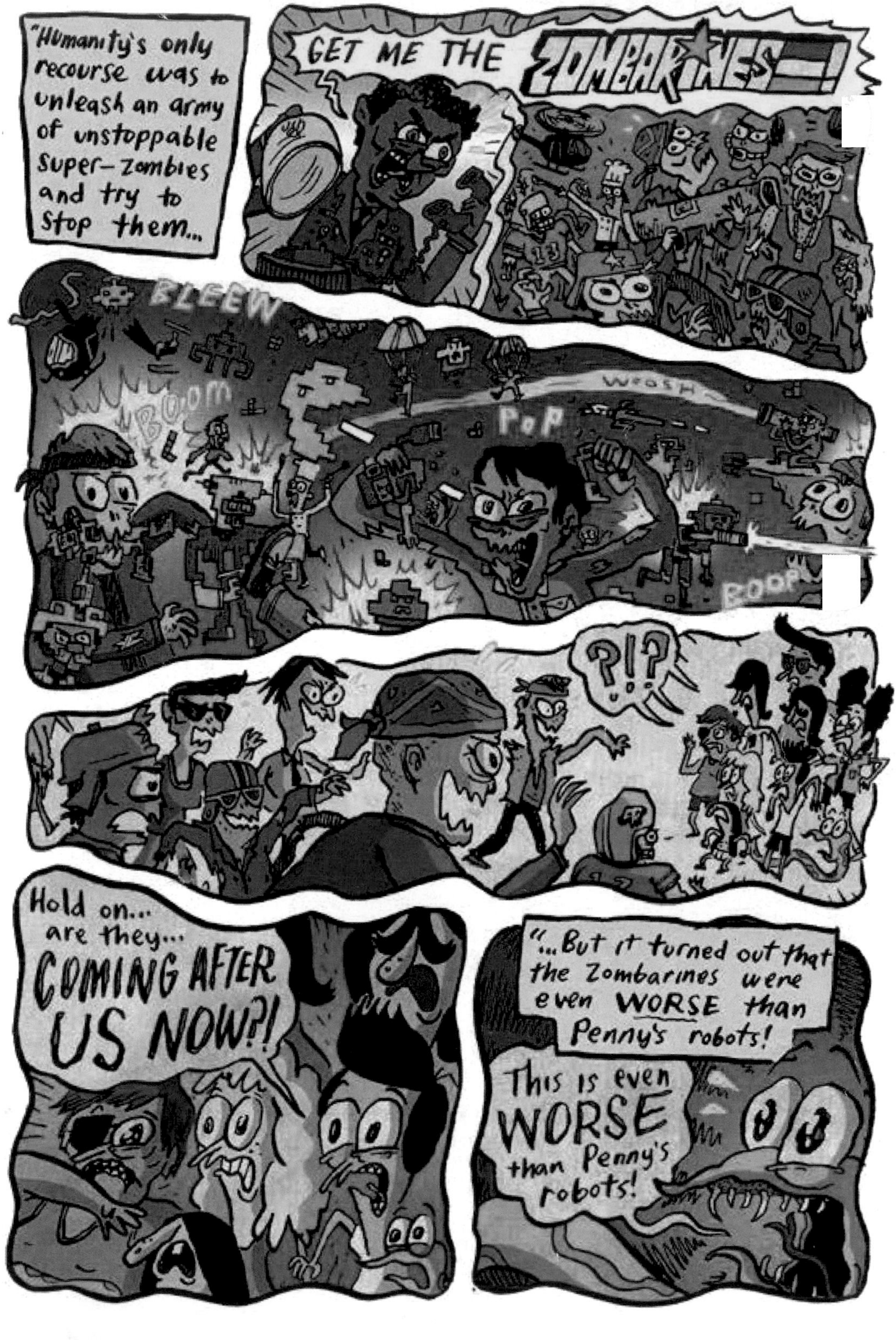

"Humanity's only recourse was to unleash an army of unstoppable super-zombies and try to stop them...
GET ME THE ZOMBARINES!
BLEEW
BOOM
POP
WOOSH
BOOP
?!?
Hold on... are they... COMING AFTER US NOW?!
"...But it turned out that the Zombarines were even WORSE than Penny's robots!
This is even WORSE than Penny's robots!

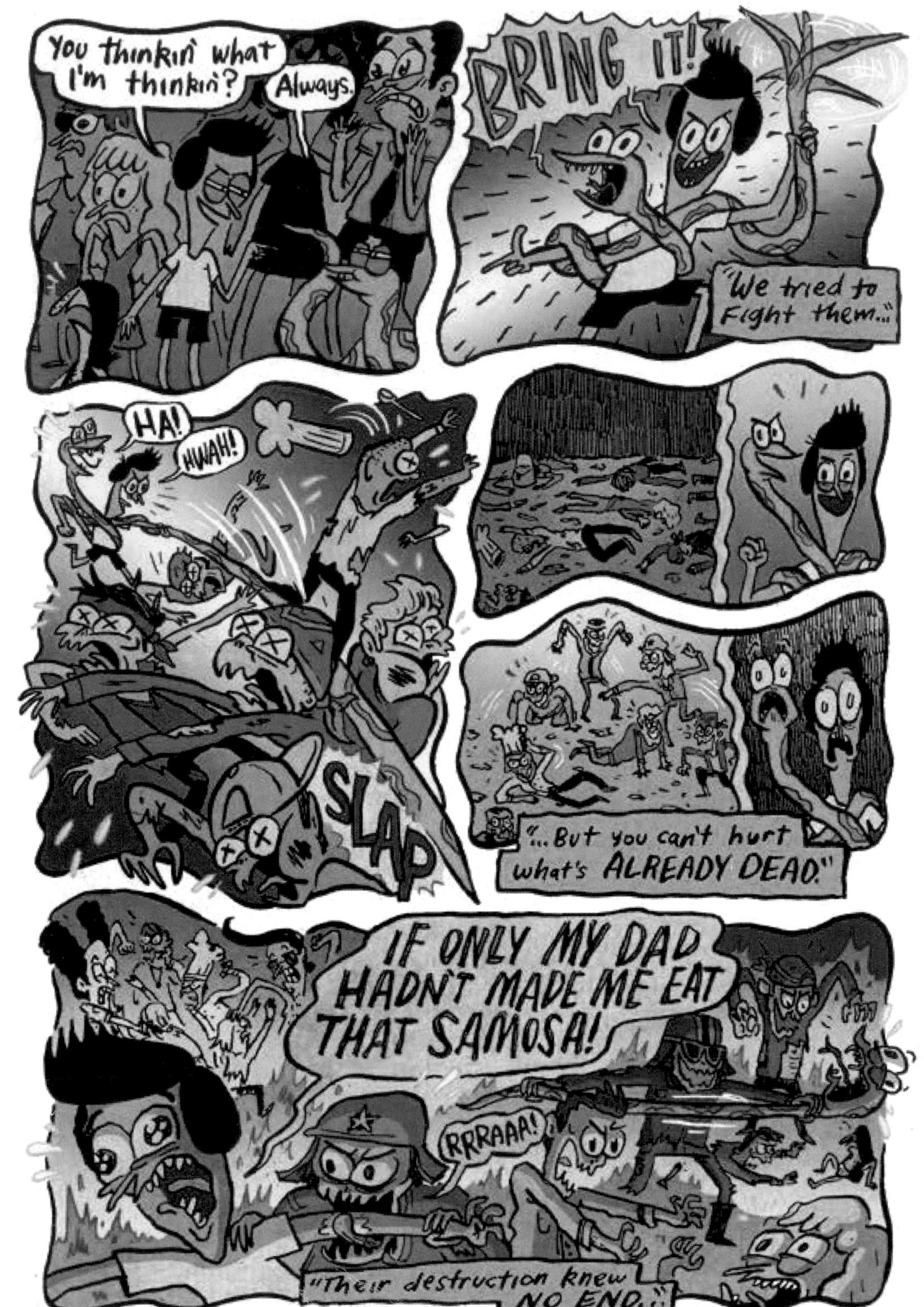
You thinkin' what I'm thinkin'?
Always.
BRING IT!
"We tried to Fight them..."
HA!
HWAH!
SLAP
"...But you can't hurt what's ALREADY DEAD."
IF ONLY MY DAD HADN'T MADE ME EAT THAT SAMOSA!
RRRAAA!
"Their destruction knew NO END..."

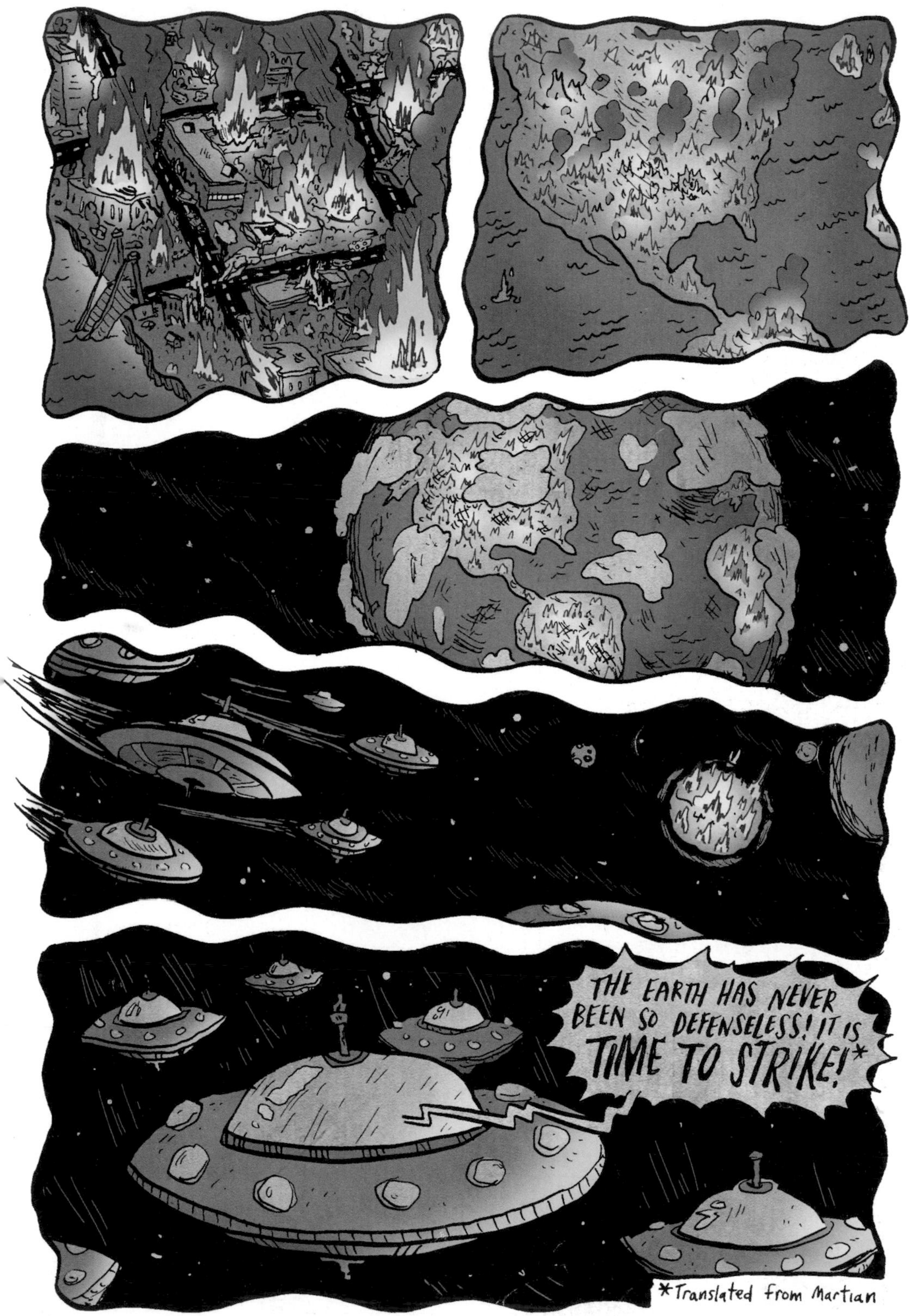
THE EARTH HAS NEVER BEEN SO DEFENSELESS! IT IS TIME TO STRIKE!*
*Translated from Martian

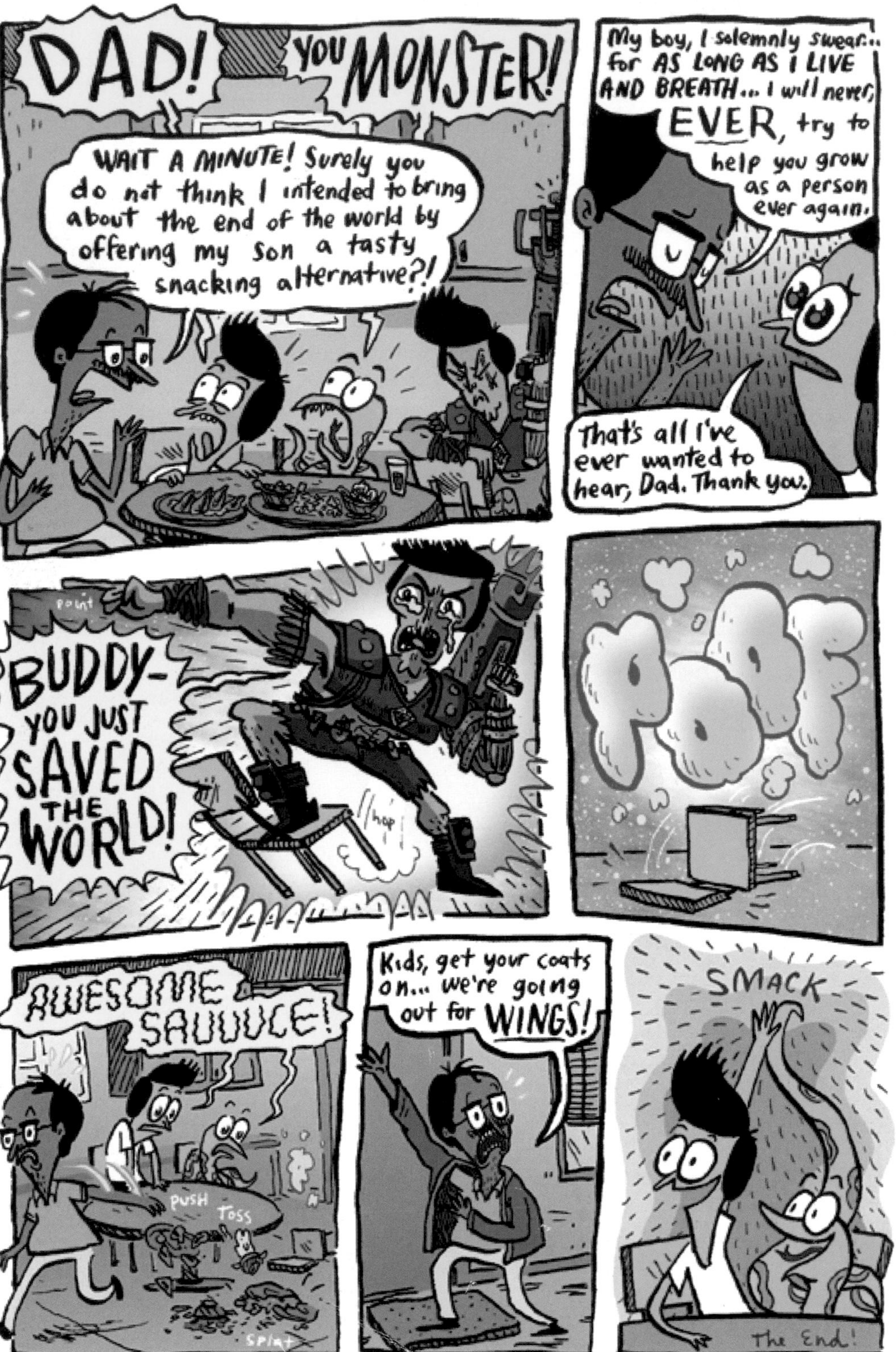
DAD! YOU MONSTER!
WAIT A MINUTE! Surely you do not think I intended to bring about the end of the world by offering my son a tasty snacking alternative?!
My boy, I solemnly swear... for AS LONG AS I LIVE AND BREATH... I will never, EVER, try to help you grow as a person ever again.
That's all I've ever wanted to hear, Dad. Thank you.
point
BUDDY- YOU JUST SAVED THE WORLD!
hop
POOF
AWESOME SAUUUCE!
PUSH
TOSS
SPlat
Kids, get your coats on... we're going out for WINGS!
SMACK
The End!

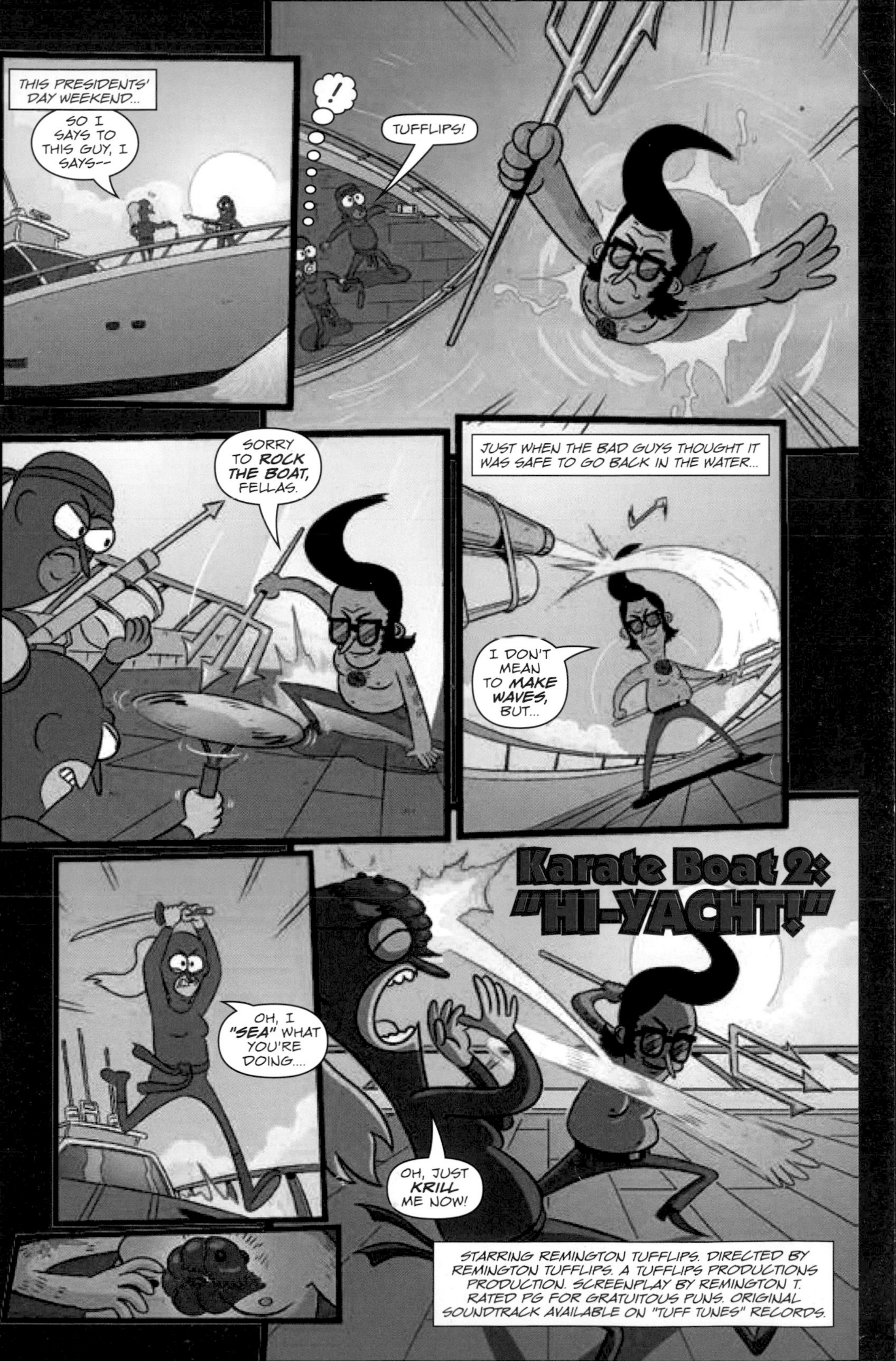
THIS PRESIDENTS' DAY WEEKEND...
SO I SAYS TO THIS GUY, I SAYS--
!
TUFFLIPS!
SORRY TO ROCK THE BOAT, FELLAS.
JUST WHEN THE BAD GUYS THOUGHT IT WAS SAFE TO GO BACK IN THE WATER...
I DON'T MEAN TO MAKE WAVES, BUT...
Karate Boat 2: "HI-YACHT!"
OH, I "SEA" WHAT YOU'RE DOING....
OH, JUST KRILL ME NOW!
STARRING REMINGTON TUFFLIPS. DIRECTED BY REMINGTON TUFFLIPS. A TUFFLIPS PRODUCTIONS PRODUCTION. SCREENPLAY BY REMINGTON T. RATED PG FOR GRATUITOUS PUNS. ORIGINAL SOUNDTRACK AVAILABLE ON "TUFF TUNES" RECORDS.

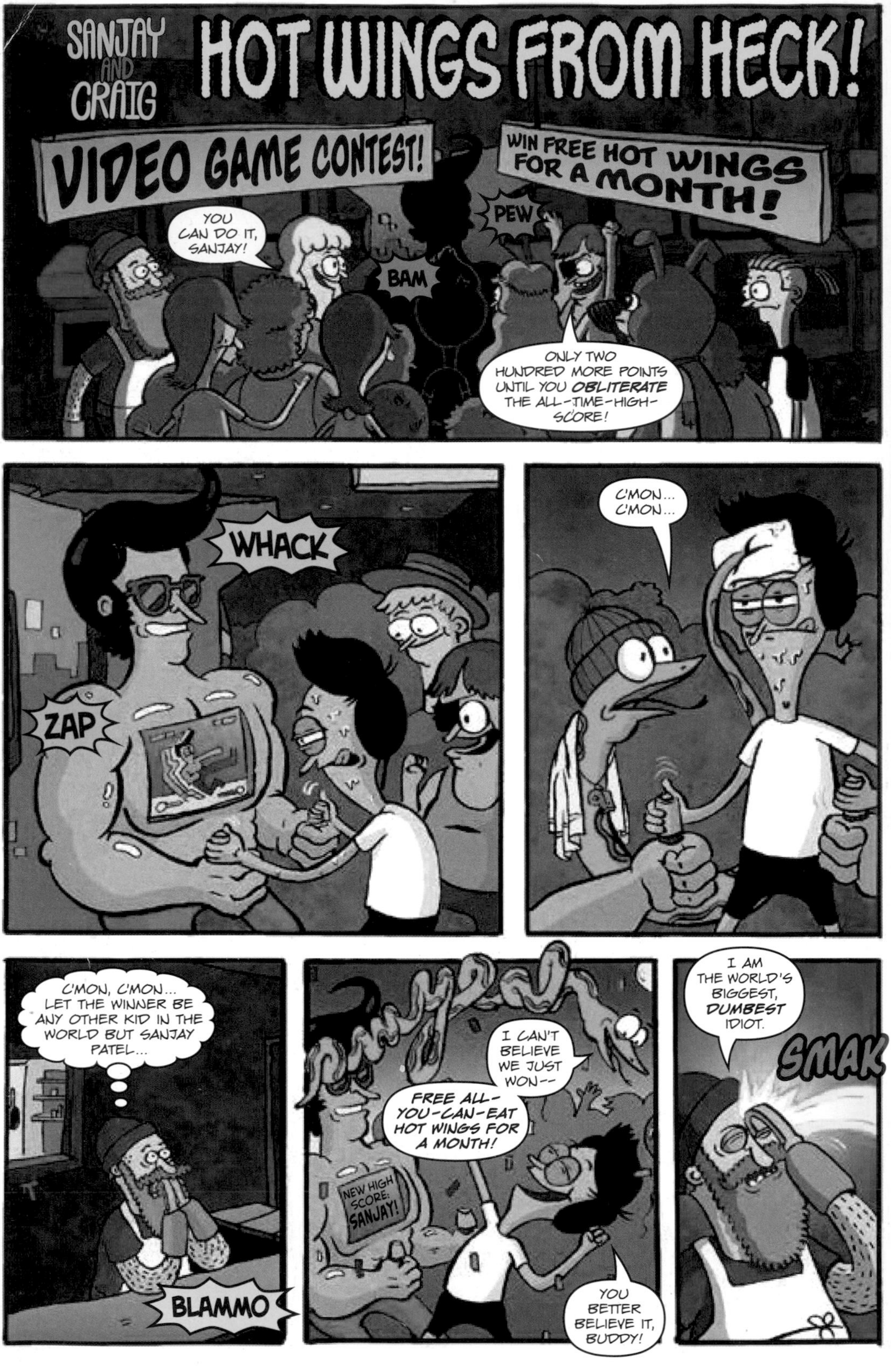
SANJAY AND CRAIG
HOT WINGS FROM HECK!
VIDEO GAME CONTEST!
WIN FREE HOT WINGS FOR A MONTH!
YOU CAN DO IT, SANJAY!
PEW
BAM
ONLY TWO HUNDRED MORE POINTS UNTIL YOU OBLITERATE THE ALL-TIME-HIGH-SCORE!
WHACK
ZAP
C'MON... C'MON...
C'MON, C'MON... LET THE WINNER BE ANY OTHER KID IN THE WORLD BUT SANJAY PATEL...
BLAMMO
I CAN'T BELIEVE WE JUST WON--
FREE ALL-YOU-CAN-EAT HOT WINGS FOR A MONTH!
NEW HIGH SCORE: SANJAY!
YOU BETTER BELIEVE IT, BUDDY!
I AM THE WORLD'S BIGGEST, DUMBEST IDIOT.
SMAK

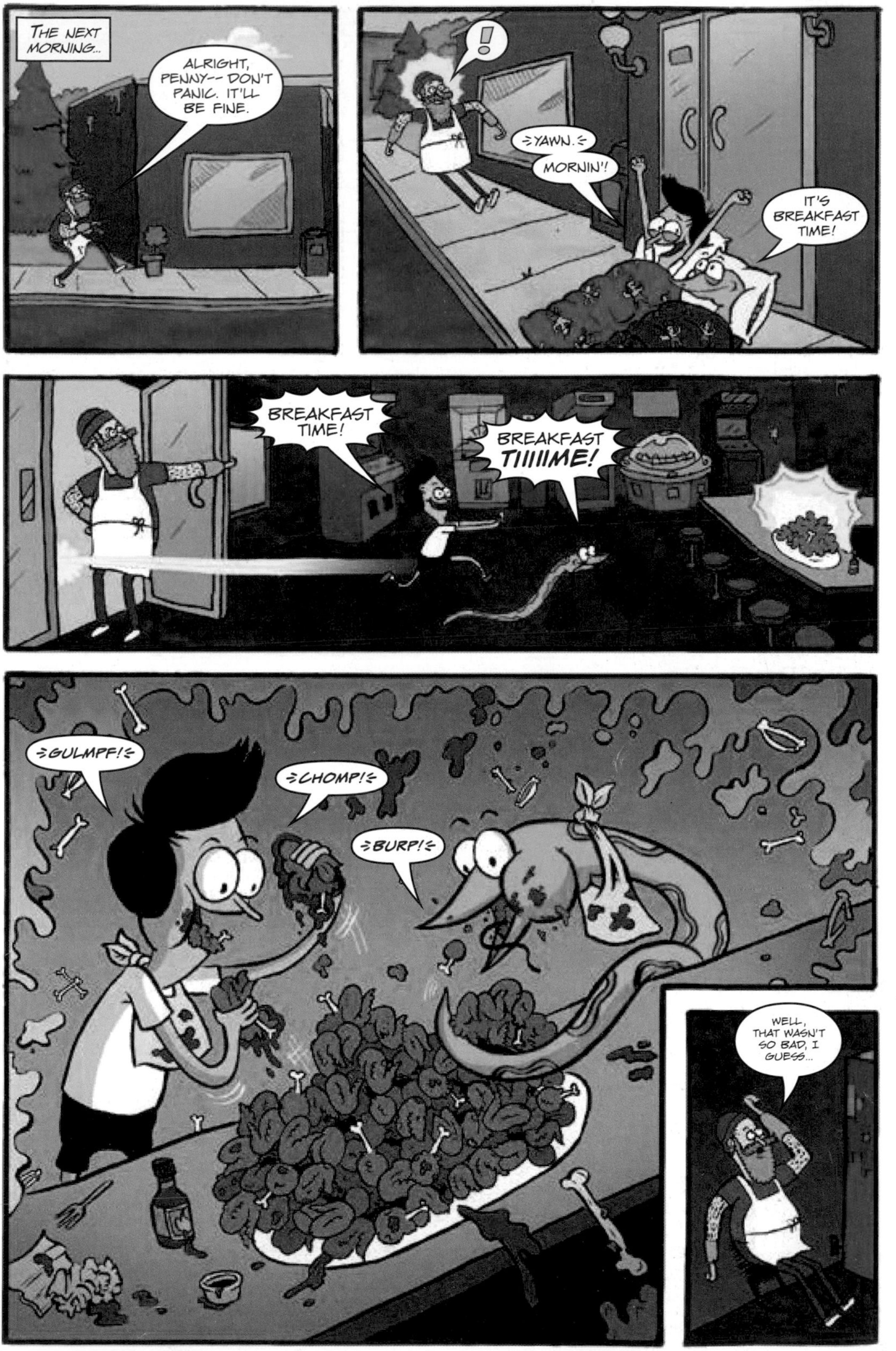
THE NEXT MORNING...
ALRIGHT, PENNY-- DON'T PANIC. IT'LL BE FINE.
!
YAWN.
MORNIN'!
IT'S BREAKFAST TIME!
BREAKFAST TIME!
BREAKFAST TIIIIIME!
GULMPF!
CHOMP!
BURP!
WELL, THAT WASN'T SO BAD, I GUESS...

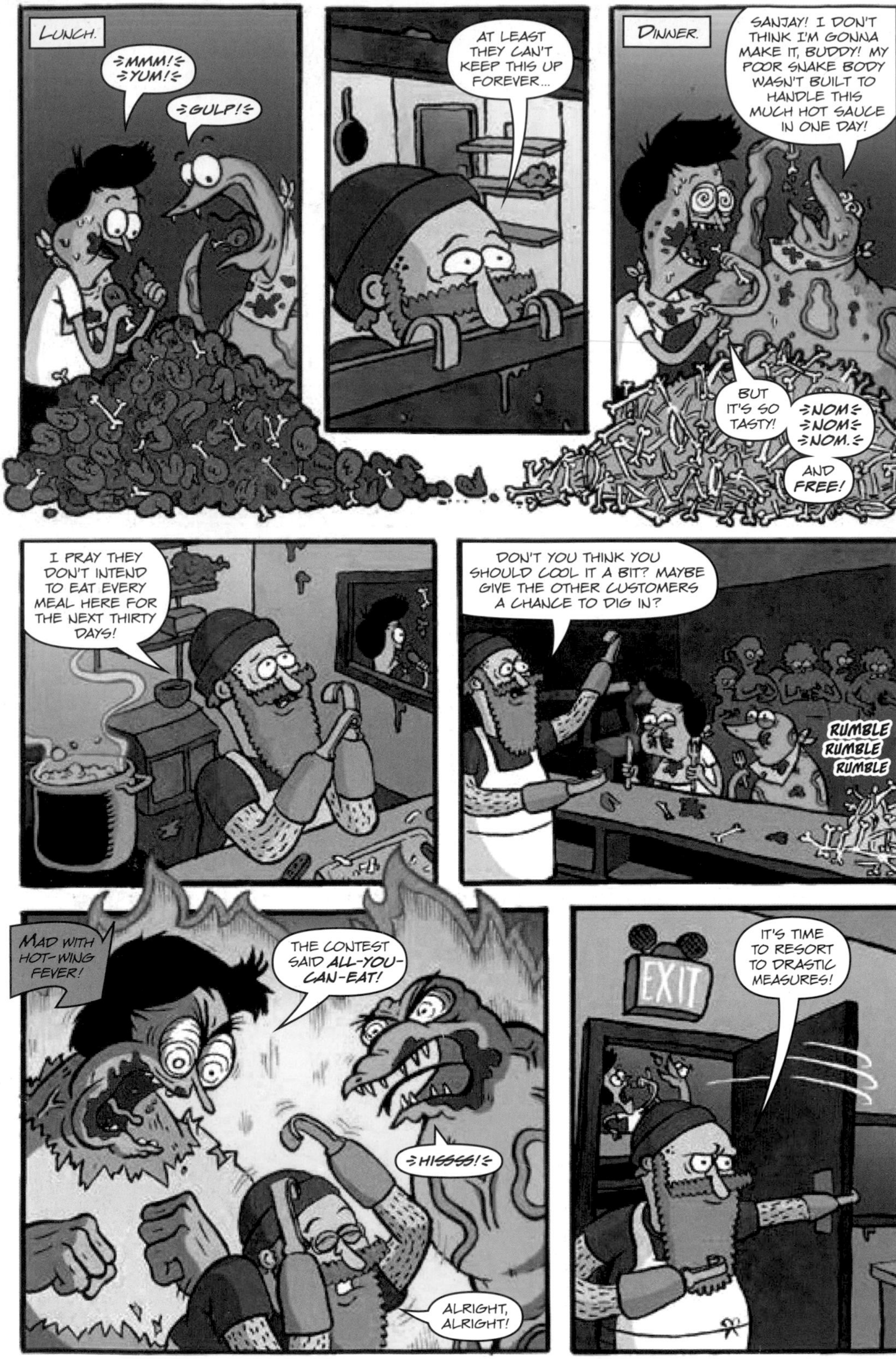
Lunch.
MMM! YUM!
GULP!
AT LEAST THEY CAN'T KEEP THIS UP FOREVER...
Dinner.
SANJAY! I DON'T THINK I'M GONNA MAKE IT, BUDDY! MY POOR SNAKE BODY WASN'T BUILT TO HANDLE THIS MUCH HOT SAUCE IN ONE DAY!
BUT IT'S SO TASTY!
NOM NOM NOM.
AND FREE!
I PRAY THEY DON'T INTEND TO EAT EVERY MEAL HERE FOR THE NEXT THIRTY DAYS!
DON'T YOU THINK YOU SHOULD COOL IT A BIT? MAYBE GIVE THE OTHER CUSTOMERS A CHANCE TO DIG IN?
RUMBLE RUMBLE RUMBLE
MAD WITH HOT-WING FEVER!
THE CONTEST SAID ALL-YOU-CAN-EAT!
HISSSS!
ALRIGHT, ALRIGHT!
EXIT
IT'S TIME TO RESORT TO DRASTIC MEASURES!

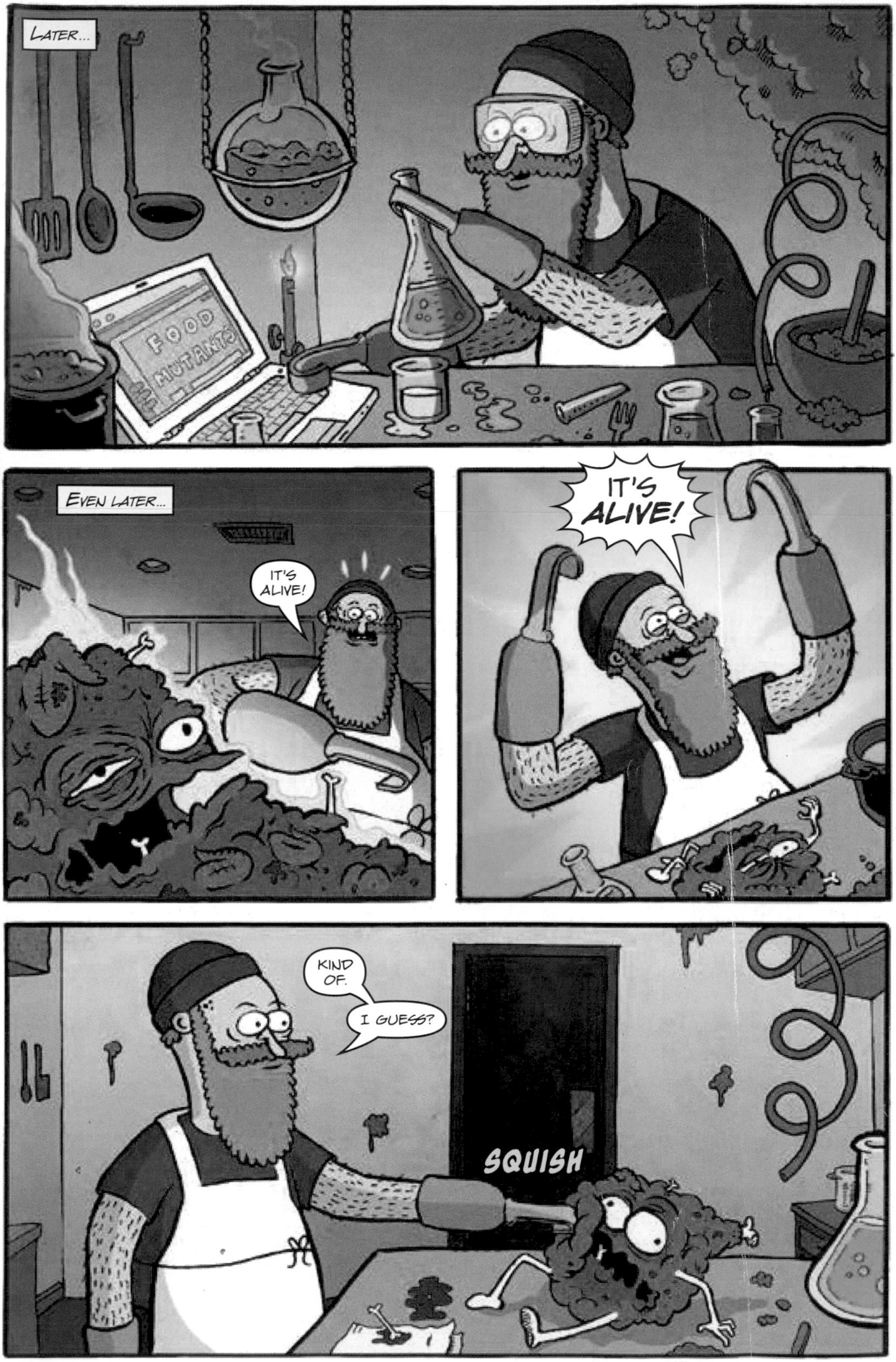
LATER...
FOOD MUTANTS
EVEN LATER...
IT'S ALIVE!
IT'S ALIVE!
KIND OF.
I GUESS?
SQUISH

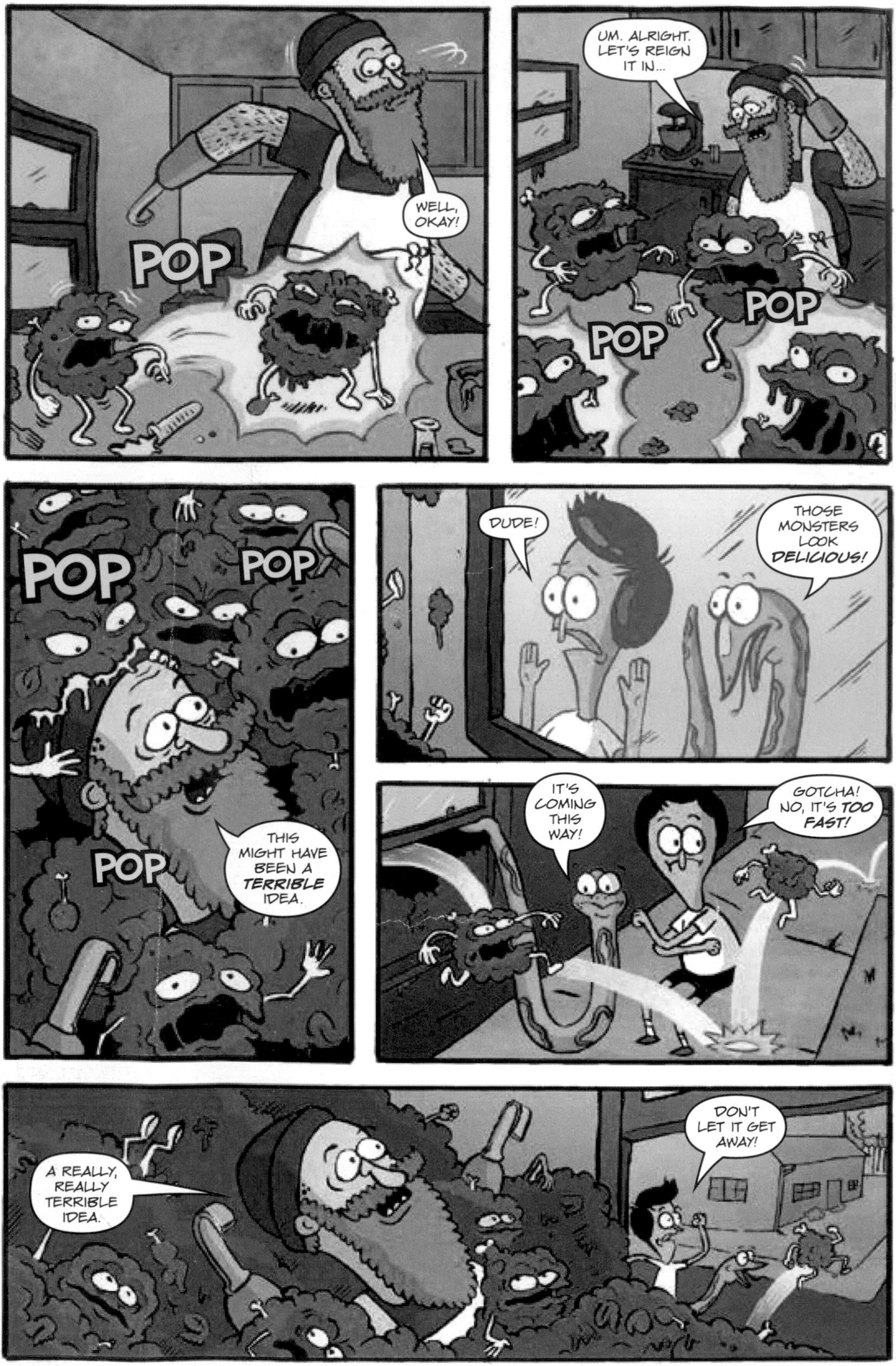
WELL, OKAY!
POP
UM. ALRIGHT. LET'S REIGN IT IN...
POP
POP
POP
POP
THIS MIGHT HAVE BEEN A TERRIBLE IDEA.
POP
DUDE!
THOSE MONSTERS LOOK DELICIOUS!
IT'S COMING THIS WAY!
GOTCHA! NO, IT'S TOO FAST!
A REALLY, REALLY TERRIBLE IDEA.
DON'T LET IT GET AWAY!

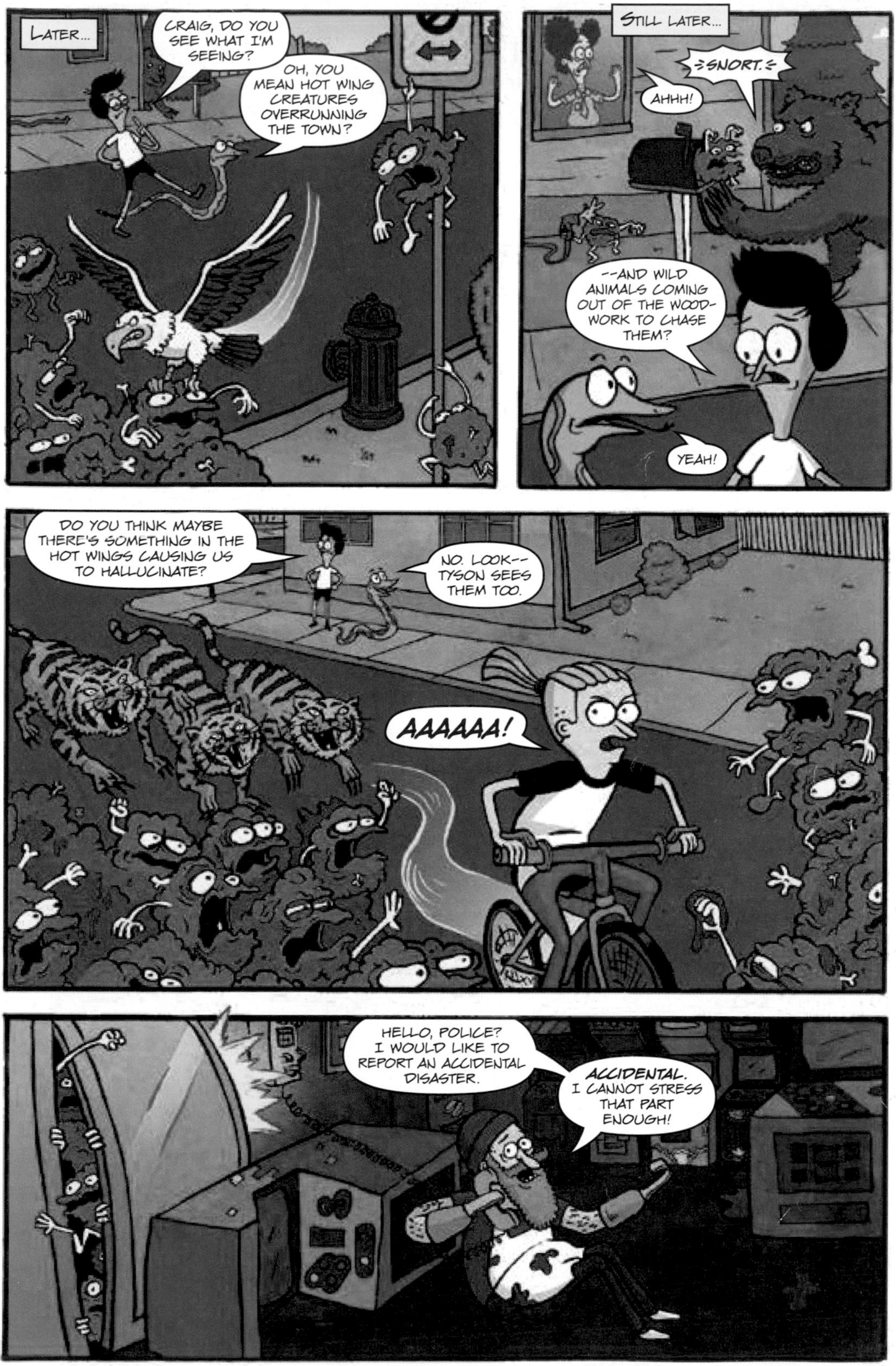
LATER...
CRAIG, DO YOU SEE WHAT I'M SEEING?
OH, YOU MEAN HOT WING CREATURES OVERRUNNING THE TOWN?
STILL LATER...
SNORT.
AHHH!
--AND WILD ANIMALS COMING OUT OF THE WOOD-WORK TO CHASE THEM?
YEAH!
DO YOU THINK MAYBE THERE'S SOMETHING IN THE HOT WINGS CAUSING US TO HALLUCINATE?
NO. LOOK-- TYSON SEES THEM TOO.
AAAAAA!
HELLO, POLICE? I WOULD LIKE TO REPORT AN ACCIDENTAL DISASTER.
ACCIDENTAL. I CANNOT STRESS THAT PART ENOUGH!

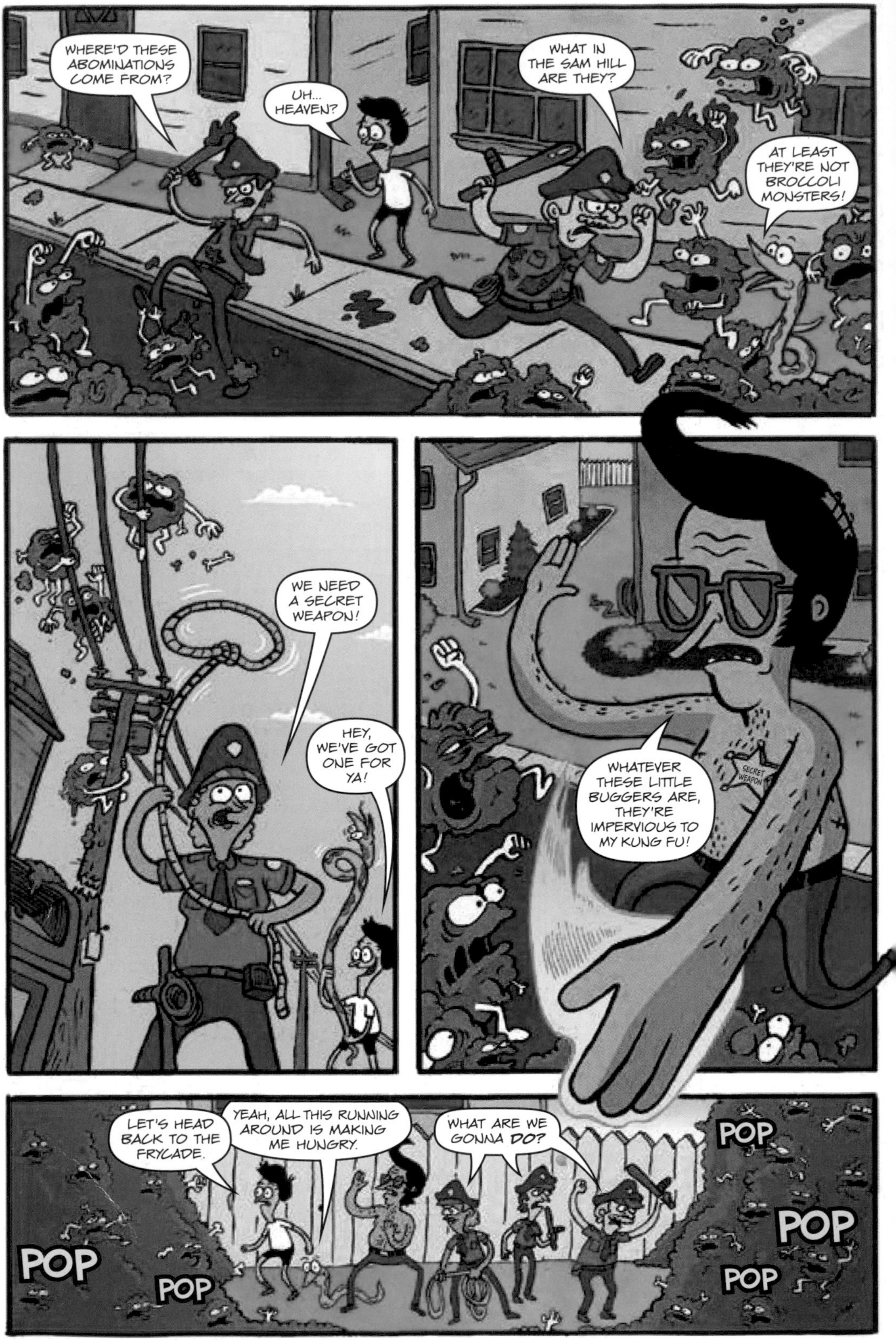
WHERE'D THESE ABOMINATIONS COME FROM?
UH... HEAVEN?
WHAT IN THE SAM HILL ARE THEY?
AT LEAST THEY'RE NOT BROCCOLI MONSTERS!
WE NEED A SECRET WEAPON!
HEY, WE'VE GOT ONE FOR YA!
SECRET WEAPON
WHATEVER THESE LITTLE BUGGERS ARE, THEY'RE IMPERVIOUS TO MY KUNG FU!
LET'S HEAD BACK TO THE FRYCADE.
YEAH, ALL THIS RUNNING AROUND IS MAKING ME HUNGRY.
WHAT ARE WE GONNA **DO?**
POP
POP
POP
POP
POP

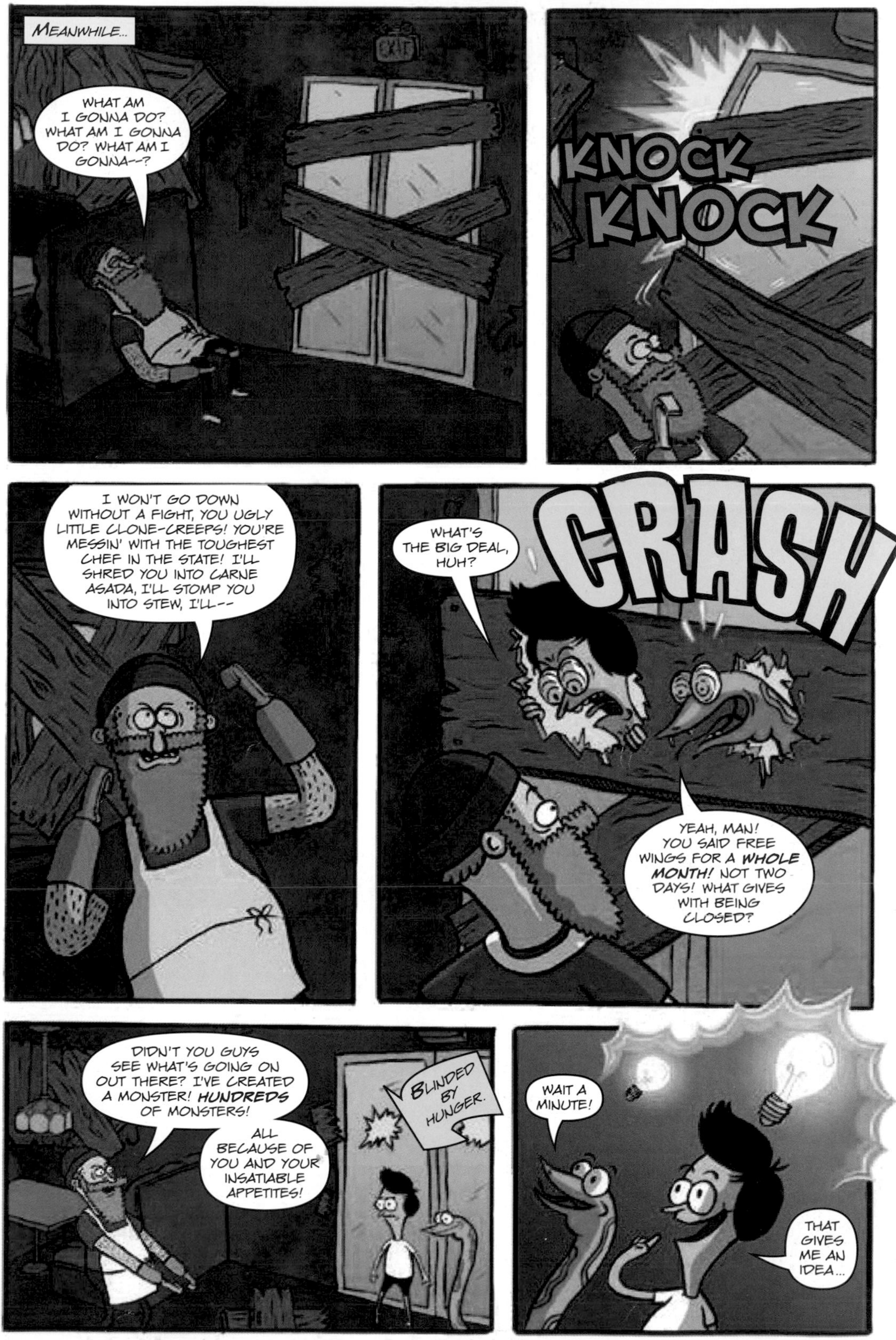
MEANWHILE...
EXIT
WHAT AM I GONNA DO? WHAT AM I GONNA DO? WHAT AM I GONNA--?
KNOCK KNOCK
I WON'T GO DOWN WITHOUT A FIGHT, YOU UGLY LITTLE CLONE-CREEPS! YOU'RE MESSIN' WITH THE TOUGHEST CHEF IN THE STATE! I'LL SHRED YOU INTO CARNE ASADA, I'LL STOMP YOU INTO STEW, I'LL--
CRASH
WHAT'S THE BIG DEAL, HUH?
YEAH, MAN! YOU SAID FREE WINGS FOR A **WHOLE MONTH!** NOT TWO DAYS! WHAT GIVES WITH BEING CLOSED?
DIDN'T YOU GUYS SEE WHAT'S GOING ON OUT THERE? I'VE CREATED A MONSTER! **HUNDREDS** OF MONSTERS!
ALL BECAUSE OF YOU AND YOUR INSATIABLE APPETITES!
BLINDED BY HUNGER.
WAIT A MINUTE!
THAT GIVES ME AN IDEA...

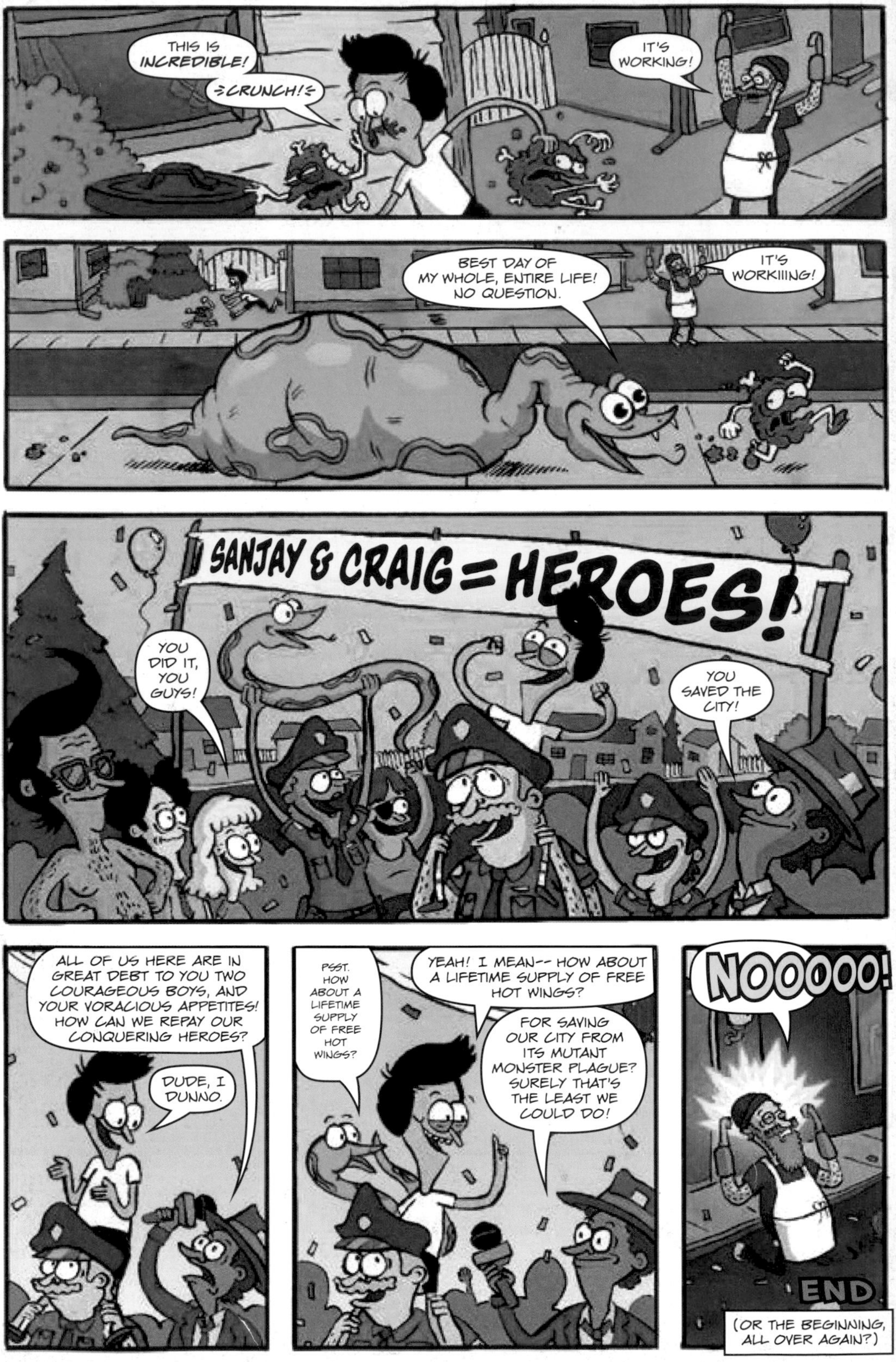

THIS IS INCREDIBLE!
CRUNCH!
IT'S WORKING!
BEST DAY OF MY WHOLE, ENTIRE LIFE! NO QUESTION.
IT'S WORKIIING!
SANJAY & CRAIG = HEROES!
YOU DID IT, YOU GUYS!
YOU SAVED THE CITY!
ALL OF US HERE ARE IN GREAT DEBT TO YOU TWO COURAGEOUS BOYS, AND YOUR VORACIOUS APPETITES! HOW CAN WE REPAY OUR CONQUERING HEROES?
DUDE, I DUNNO.
PSST. HOW ABOUT A LIFETIME SUPPLY OF FREE HOT WINGS?
YEAH! I MEAN-- HOW ABOUT A LIFETIME SUPPLY OF FREE HOT WINGS?
FOR SAVING OUR CITY FROM ITS MUTANT MONSTER PLAGUE? SURELY THAT'S THE LEAST WE COULD DO!
NOOOOO!
END
(OR THE BEGINNING, ALL OVER AGAIN?)

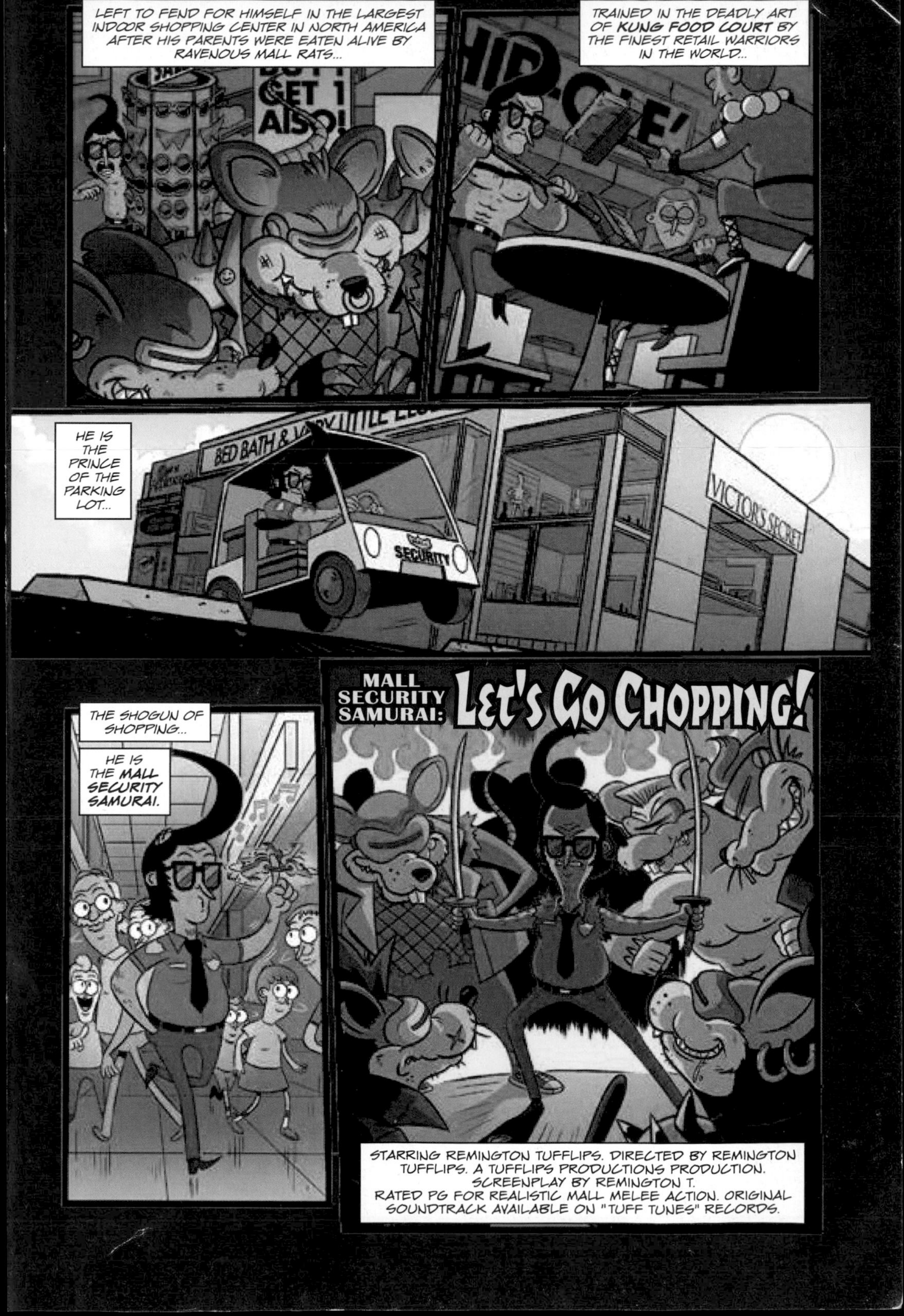
LEFT TO FEND FOR HIMSELF IN THE LARGEST INDOOR SHOPPING CENTER IN NORTH AMERICA AFTER HIS PARENTS WERE EATEN ALIVE BY RAVENOUS MALL RATS...
GET 1
TRAINED IN THE DEADLY ART OF **KUNG FOOD COURT** BY THE FINEST RETAIL WARRIORS IN THE WORLD...
HE IS THE PRINCE OF THE PARKING LOT...
SECURITY
VICTOR'S SECRET
THE SHOGUN OF SHOPPING...
HE IS THE ***MALL SECURITY SAMURAI.***
MALL SECURITY SAMURAI: LET'S GO CHOPPING!
STARRING REMINGTON TUFFLIPS. DIRECTED BY REMINGTON TUFFLIPS. A TUFFLIPS PRODUCTIONS PRODUCTION. SCREENPLAY BY REMINGTON T.
RATED PG FOR REALISTIC MALL MELEE ACTION. ORIGINAL SOUNDTRACK AVAILABLE ON "TUFF TUNES" RECORDS.

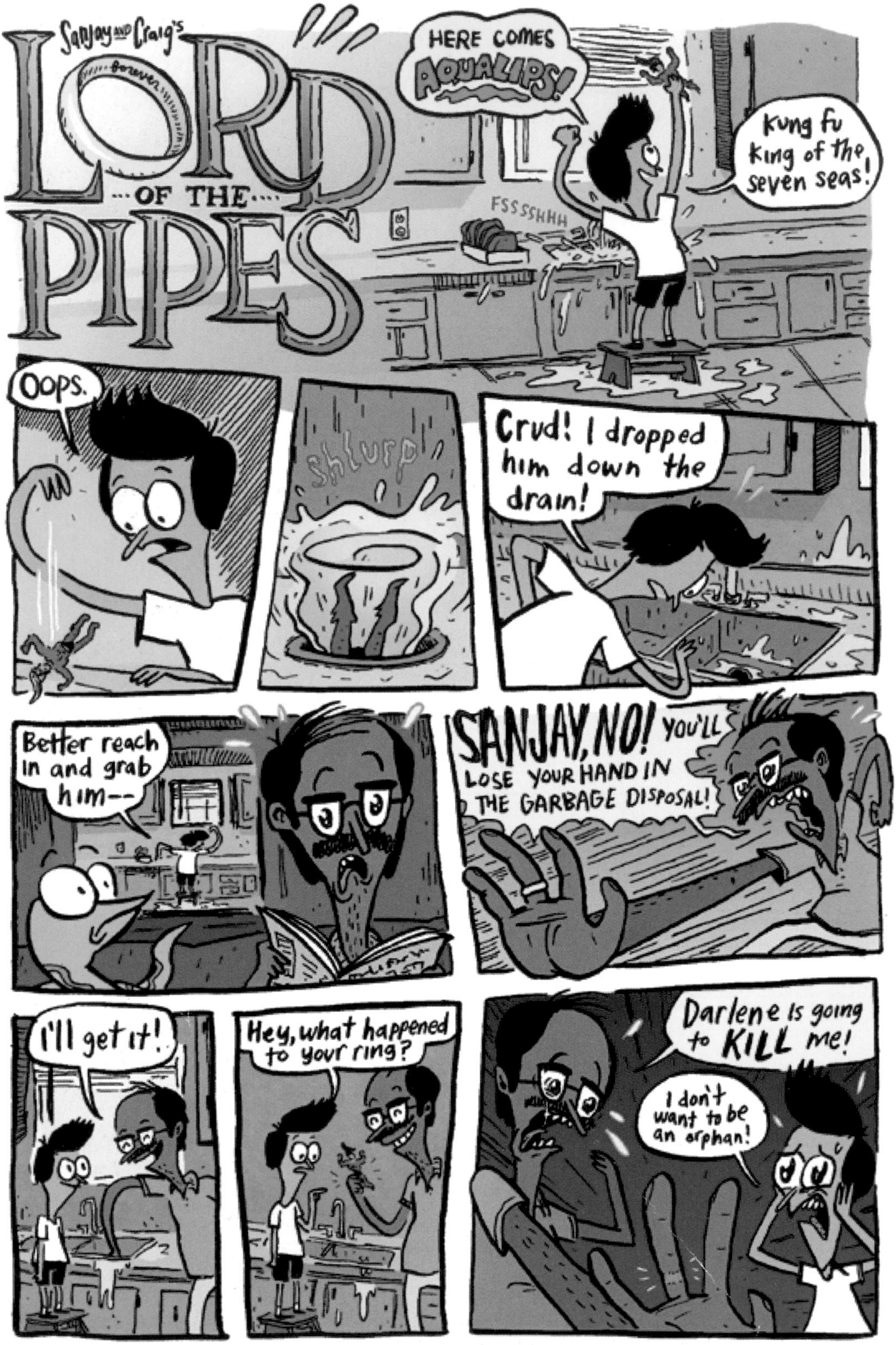

Sanjay and Craig's
LORD OF THE PIPES
forever
HERE COMES AQUALIPS!
Kung fu King of the seven seas!
FSSSSHHH
OOPS.
shlurp
Crud! I dropped him down the drain!
Better reach in and grab him--
SANJAY, NO! YOU'LL LOSE YOUR HAND IN THE GARBAGE DISPOSAL!
I'll get it!
Hey, what happened to your ring?
Darlene is going to KILL me!
I don't want to be an orphan!

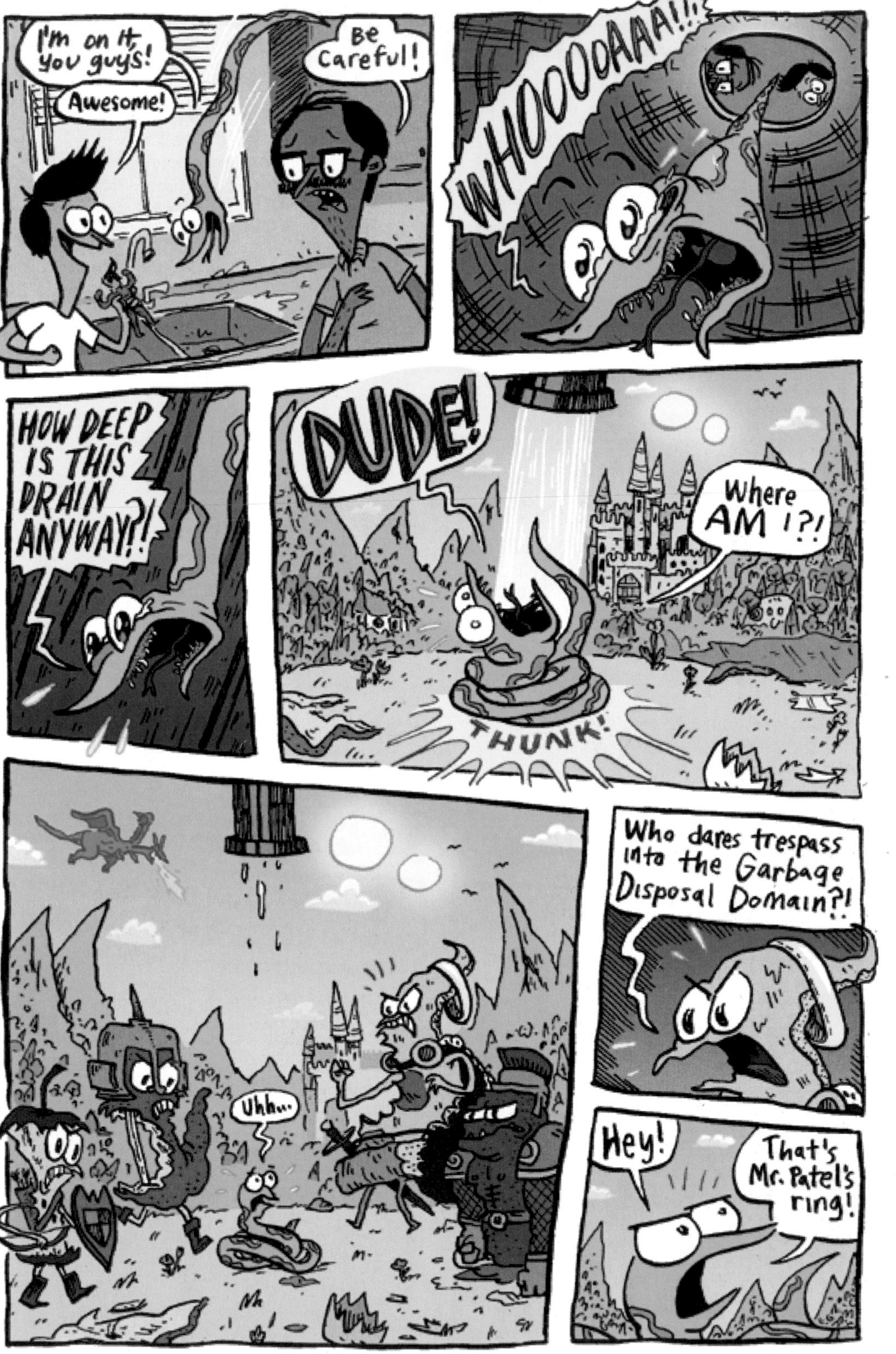
I'm on it, you guys!
Awesome!
Be Careful!
WHOOOOAAA!!!
HOW DEEP IS THIS DRAIN ANYWAY?!
DUDE!
Where AM I?!
THUNK!
Uhh...
Who dares trespass into the Garbage Disposal Domain?!
Hey!
That's Mr. Patel's ring!

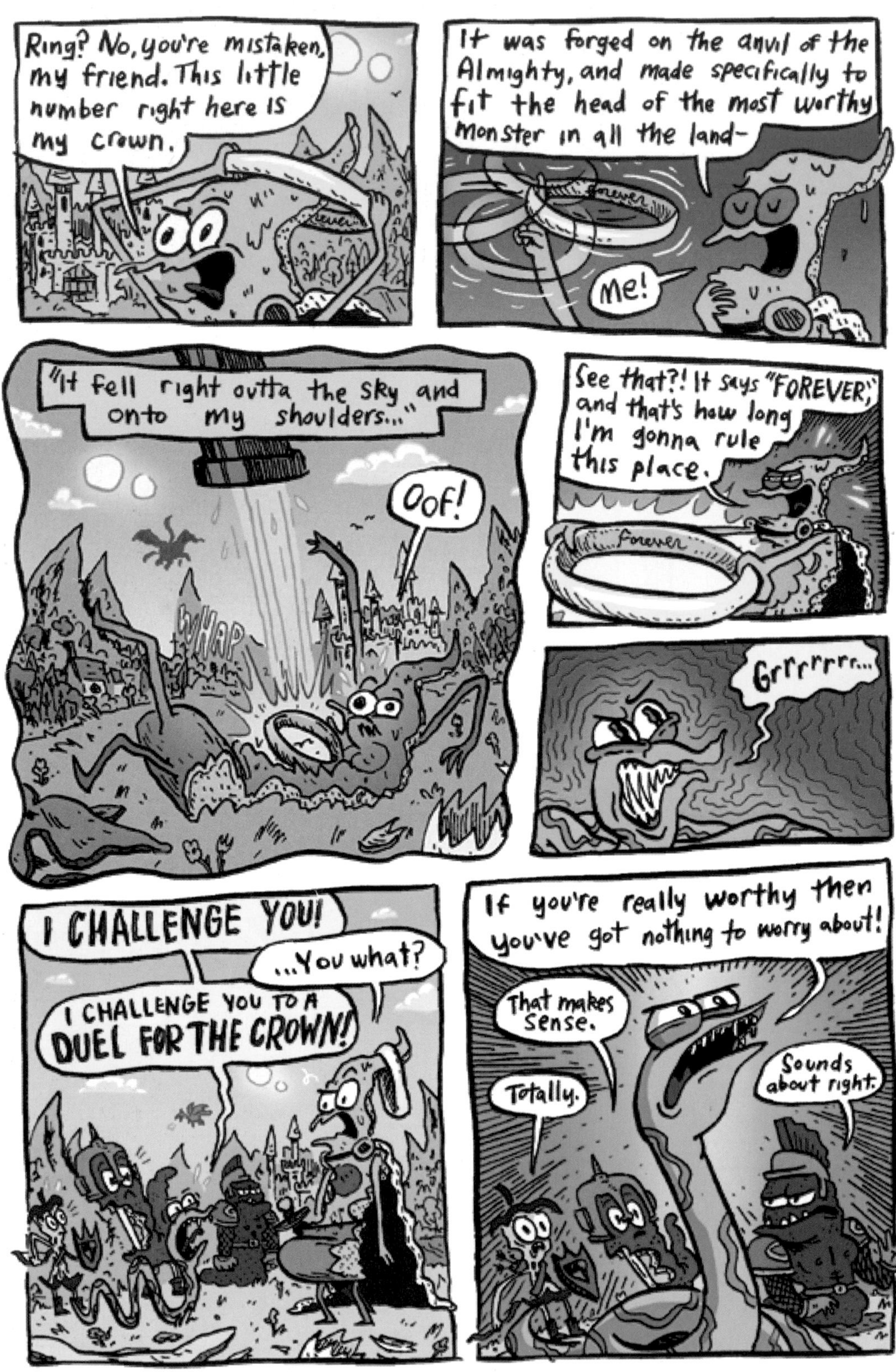
Ring? No, you're mistaken, my friend. This little number right here is my crown.
Forever
It was forged on the anvil of the Almighty, and made specifically to fit the head of the most worthy monster in all the land–
Forever
Me!
"It fell right outta the sky and onto my shoulders..."
Oof!
WHAP
See that?! It says "FOREVER," and that's how long I'm gonna rule this place.
Forever
Grrrrrr...
I CHALLENGE YOU!
...You what?
I CHALLENGE YOU TO A DUEL FOR THE CROWN!
If you're really worthy then you've got nothing to worry about!
That makes sense.
Totally.
Sounds about right.

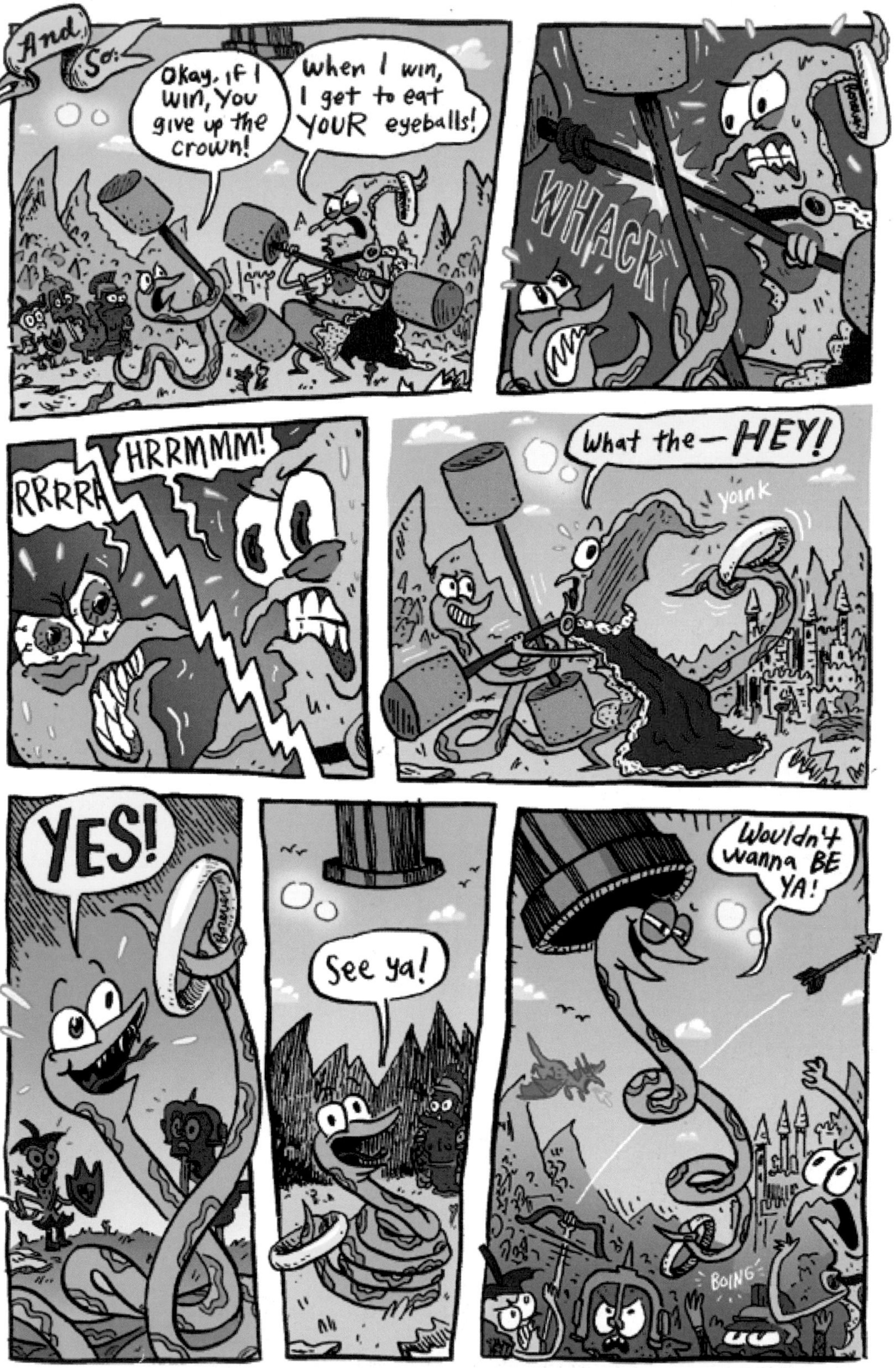
And So:
Okay, if I win, You give up the crown!
When I win, I get to eat YOUR eyeballs!
WHACK
RRRRA
HRRMMM!
What the—HEY!
yoink
YES!
See ya!
Wouldn't wanna BE YA!
BOING

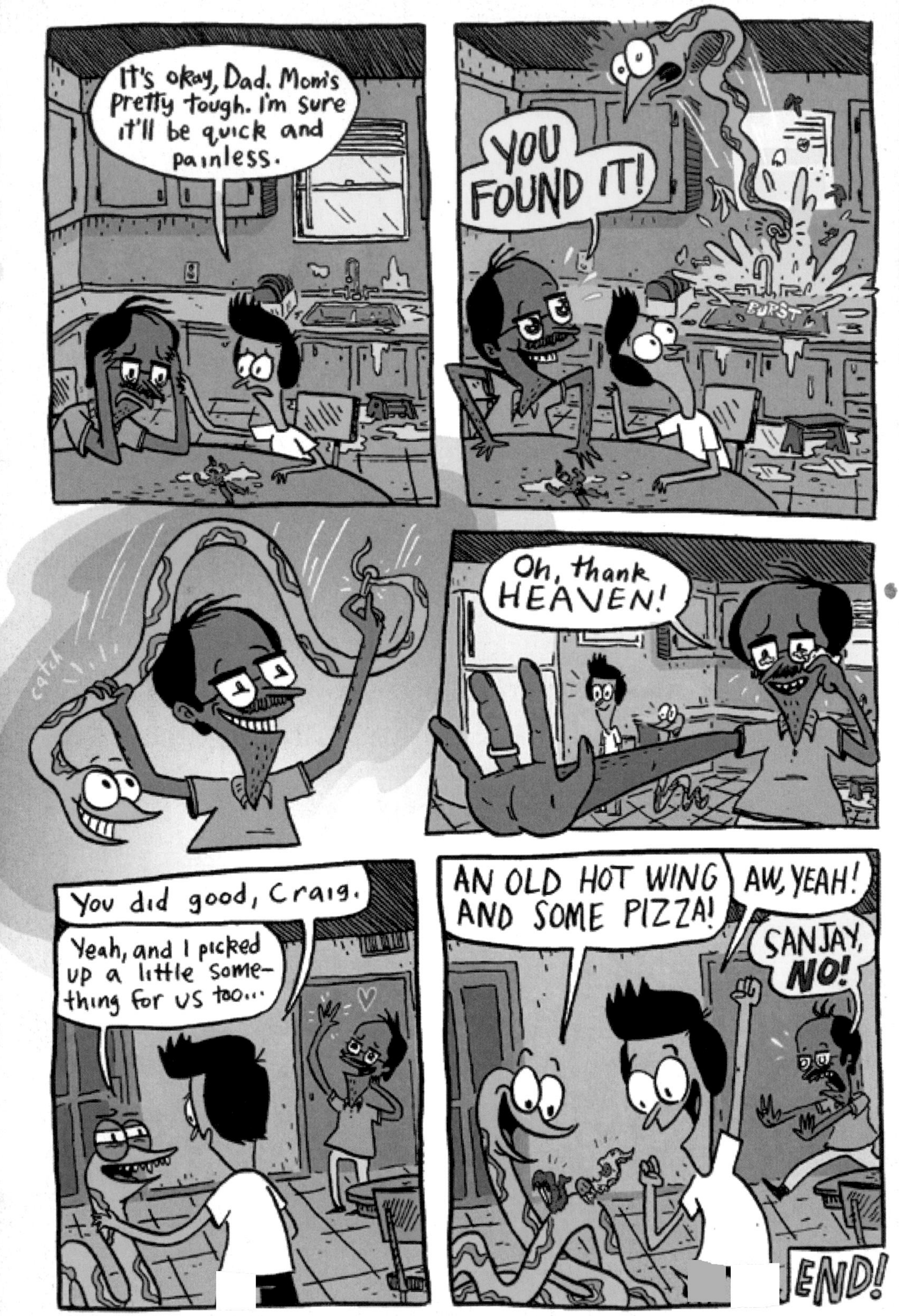
It's okay, Dad. Mom's pretty tough. I'm sure it'll be quick and painless.
YOU FOUND IT!
BURST
catch
Oh, thank HEAVEN!
You did good, Craig.
Yeah, and I picked up a little something for us too...
AN OLD HOT WING AND SOME PIZZA!
AW, YEAH!
SANJAY, NO!
END!

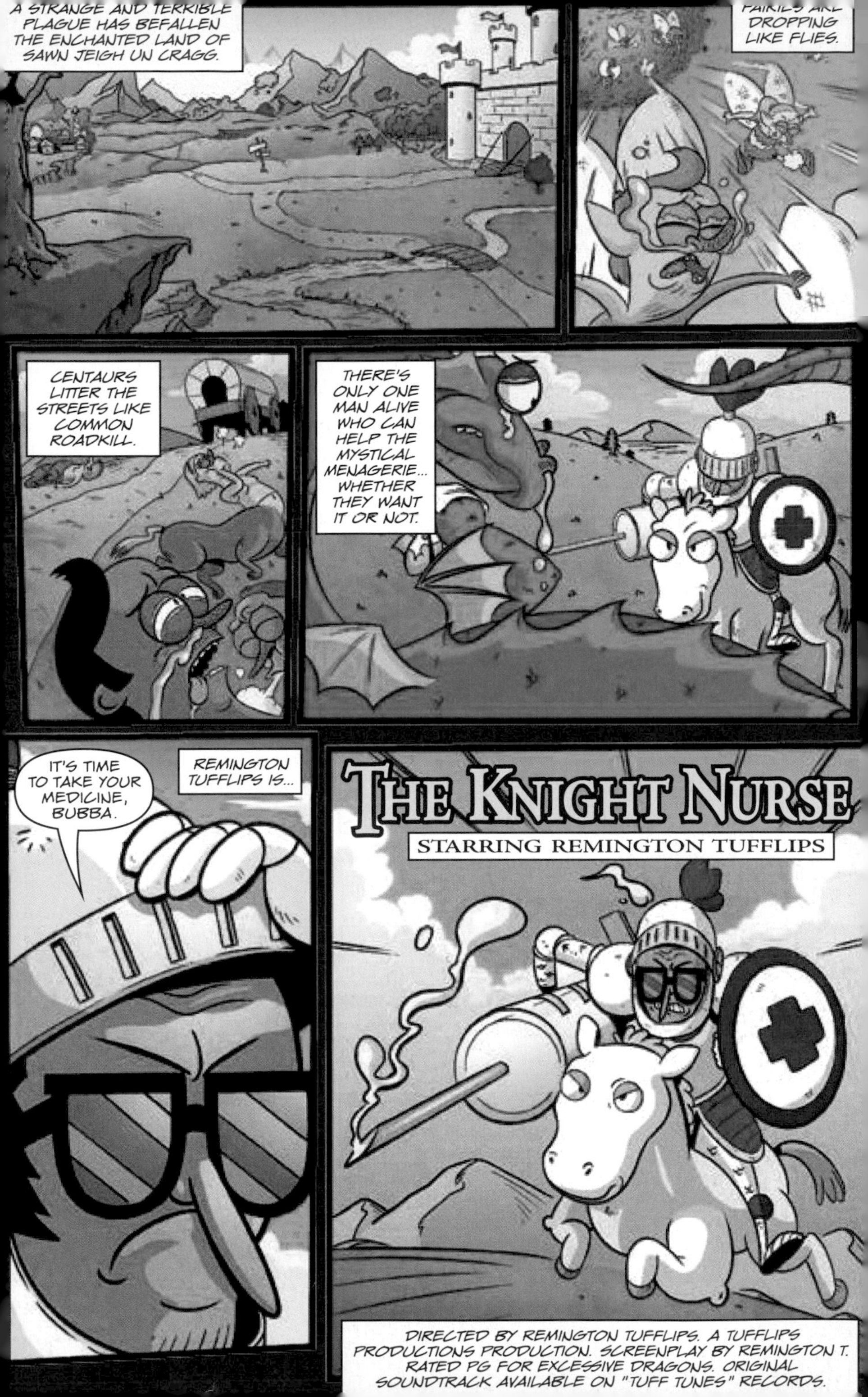
A STRANGE AND TERRIBLE PLAGUE HAS BEFALLEN THE ENCHANTED LAND OF SAWN JEIGH UN CRAGG.
FAIRIES ARE DROPPING LIKE FLIES.
CENTAURS LITTER THE STREETS LIKE COMMON ROADKILL.
THERE'S ONLY ONE MAN ALIVE WHO CAN HELP THE MYSTICAL MENAGERIE... WHETHER THEY WANT IT OR NOT.
IT'S TIME TO TAKE YOUR MEDICINE, BUBBA.
REMINGTON TUFFLIPS IS...
THE KNIGHT NURSE
STARRING REMINGTON TUFFLIPS
DIRECTED BY REMINGTON TUFFLIPS. A TUFFLIPS PRODUCTIONS PRODUCTION. SCREENPLAY BY REMINGTON T. RATED PG FOR EXCESSIVE DRAGONS. ORIGINAL SOUNDTRACK AVAILABLE ON "TUFF TUNES" RECORDS.

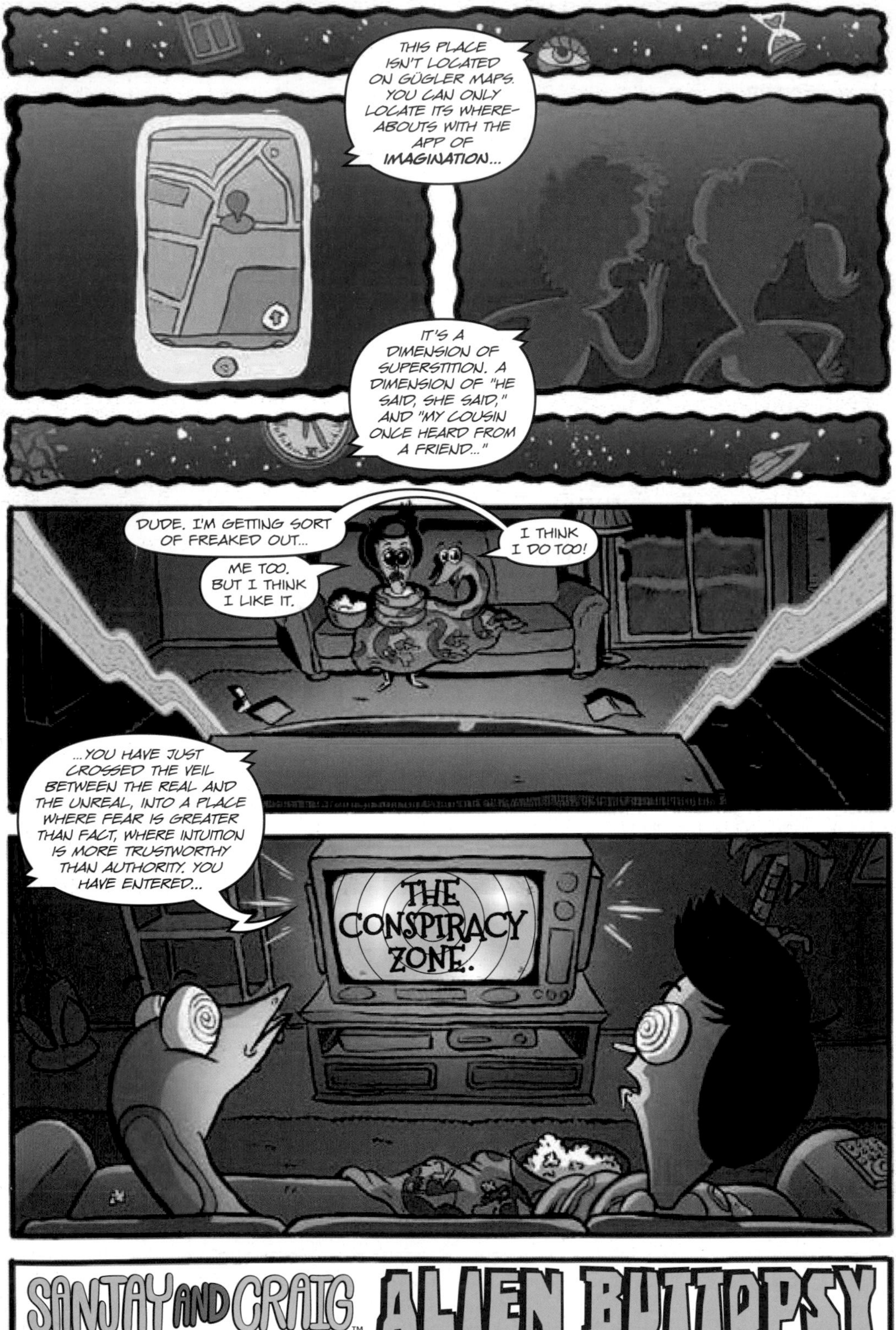
THIS PLACE ISN'T LOCATED ON GÜGLER MAPS. YOU CAN ONLY LOCATE ITS WHERE-ABOUTS WITH THE APP OF IMAGINATION...
IT'S A DIMENSION OF SUPERSTITION. A DIMENSION OF "HE SAID, SHE SAID," AND "MY COUSIN ONCE HEARD FROM A FRIEND..."
DUDE. I'M GETTING SORT OF FREAKED OUT...
ME TOO. BUT I THINK I LIKE IT.
I THINK I DO TOO!
...YOU HAVE JUST CROSSED THE VEIL BETWEEN THE REAL AND THE UNREAL, INTO A PLACE WHERE FEAR IS GREATER THAN FACT, WHERE INTUITION IS MORE TRUSTWORTHY THAN AUTHORITY. YOU HAVE ENTERED...
THE CONSPIRACY ZONE.
SANJAY AND CRAIG™ ALIEN BUTTOPSY

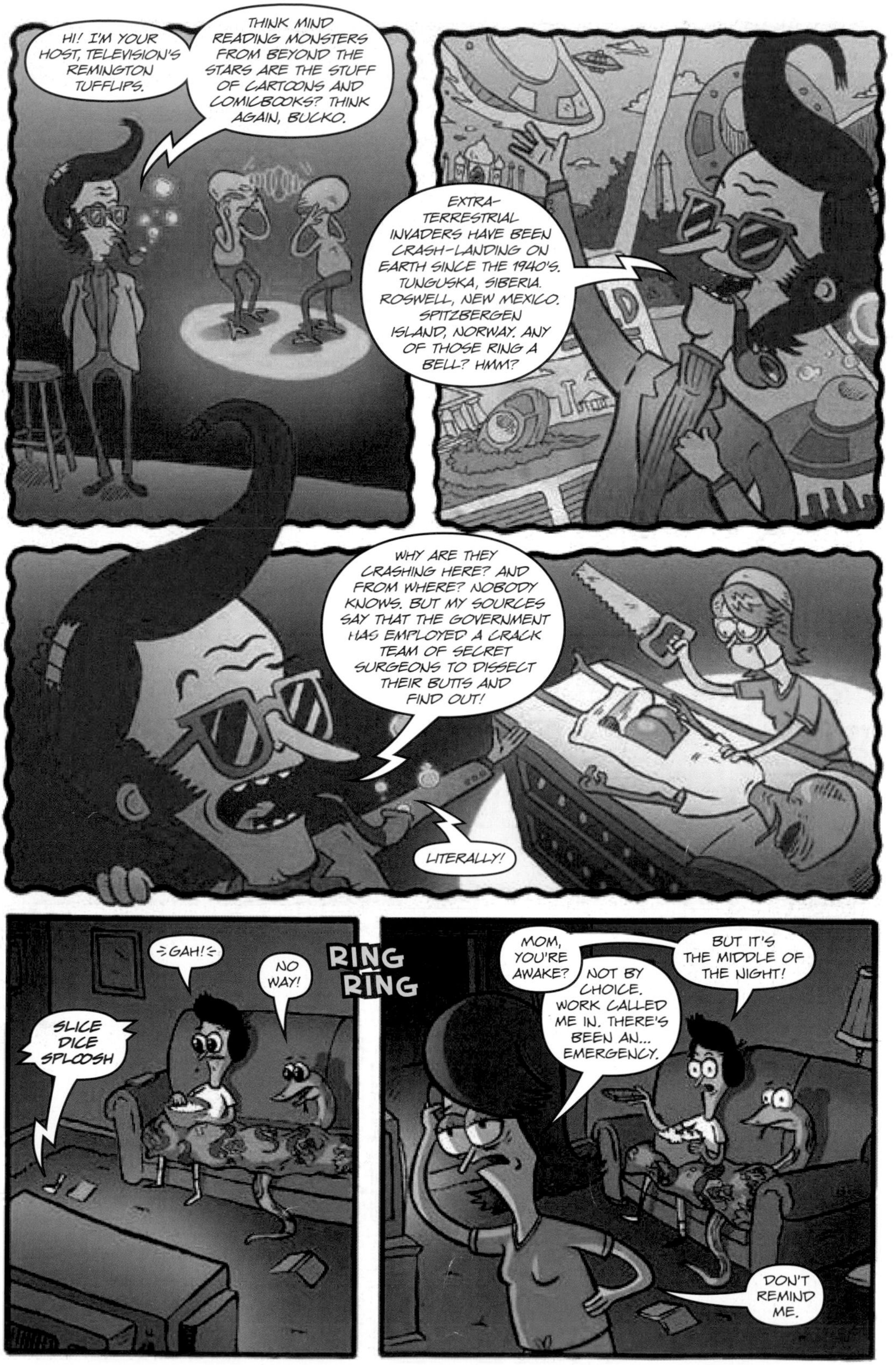
HI! I'M YOUR HOST, TELEVISION'S REMINGTON TUFFLIPS.
THINK MIND READING MONSTERS FROM BEYOND THE STARS ARE THE STUFF OF CARTOONS AND COMICBOOKS? THINK AGAIN, BUCKO.
EXTRA-TERRESTRIAL INVADERS HAVE BEEN CRASH-LANDING ON EARTH SINCE THE 1940'S. TUNGUSKA, SIBERIA. ROSWELL, NEW MEXICO. SPITZBERGEN ISLAND, NORWAY. ANY OF THOSE RING A BELL? HMM?
WHY ARE THEY CRASHING HERE? AND FROM WHERE? NOBODY KNOWS. BUT MY SOURCES SAY THAT THE GOVERNMENT HAS EMPLOYED A CRACK TEAM OF SECRET SURGEONS TO DISSECT THEIR BUTTS AND FIND OUT!
LITERALLY!
SLICE DICE SPLOOSH
GAH!
NO WAY!
RING RING
MOM, YOU'RE AWAKE?
BUT IT'S THE MIDDLE OF THE NIGHT!
NOT BY CHOICE. WORK CALLED ME IN. THERE'S BEEN AN... EMERGENCY.
DON'T REMIND ME.

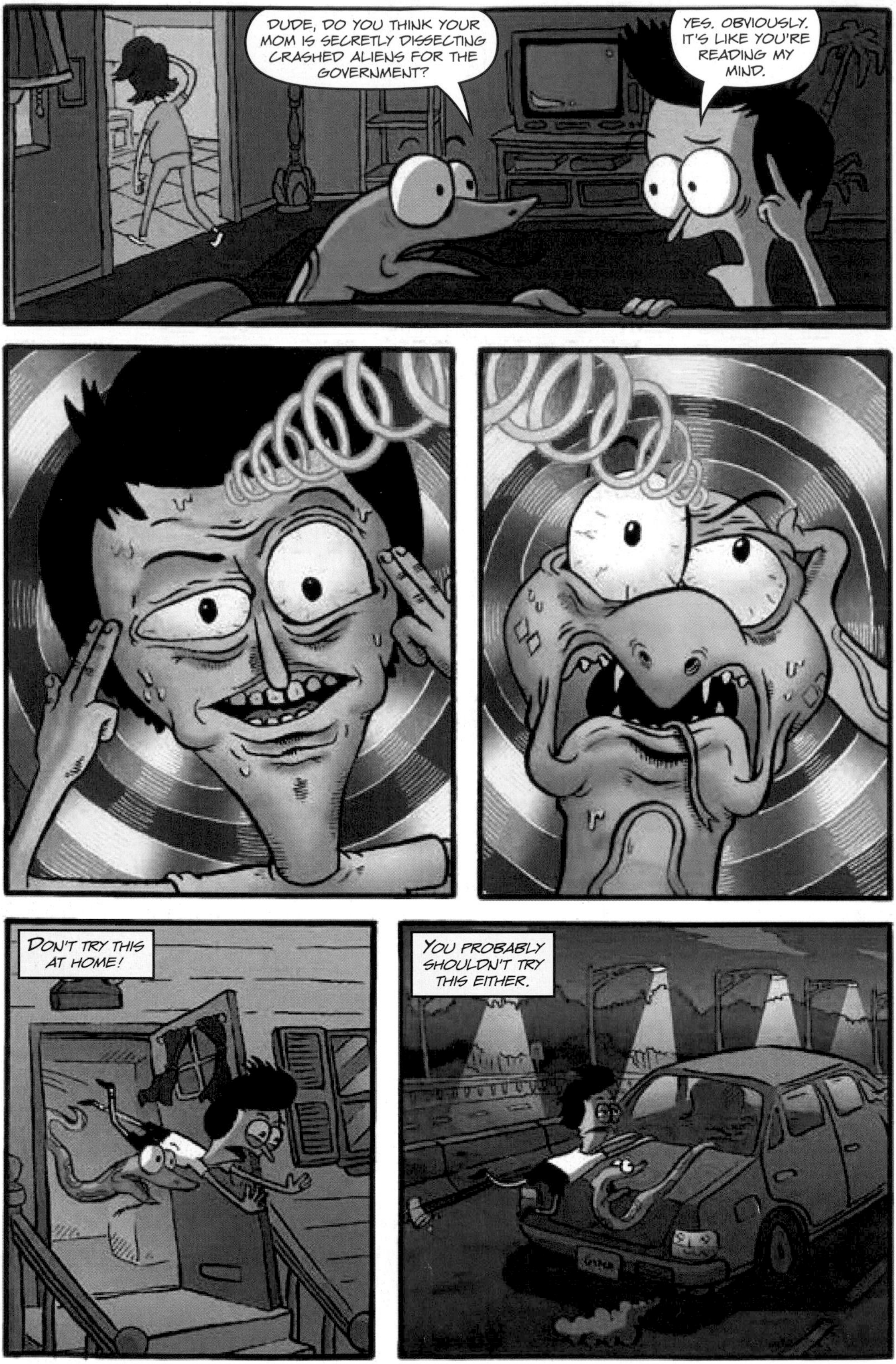
DUDE, DO YOU THINK YOUR MOM IS SECRETLY DISSECTING CRASHED ALIENS FOR THE GOVERNMENT?
YES. OBVIOUSLY. IT'S LIKE YOU'RE READING MY MIND.
DON'T TRY THIS AT HOME!
YOU PROBABLY SHOULDN'T TRY THIS EITHER.

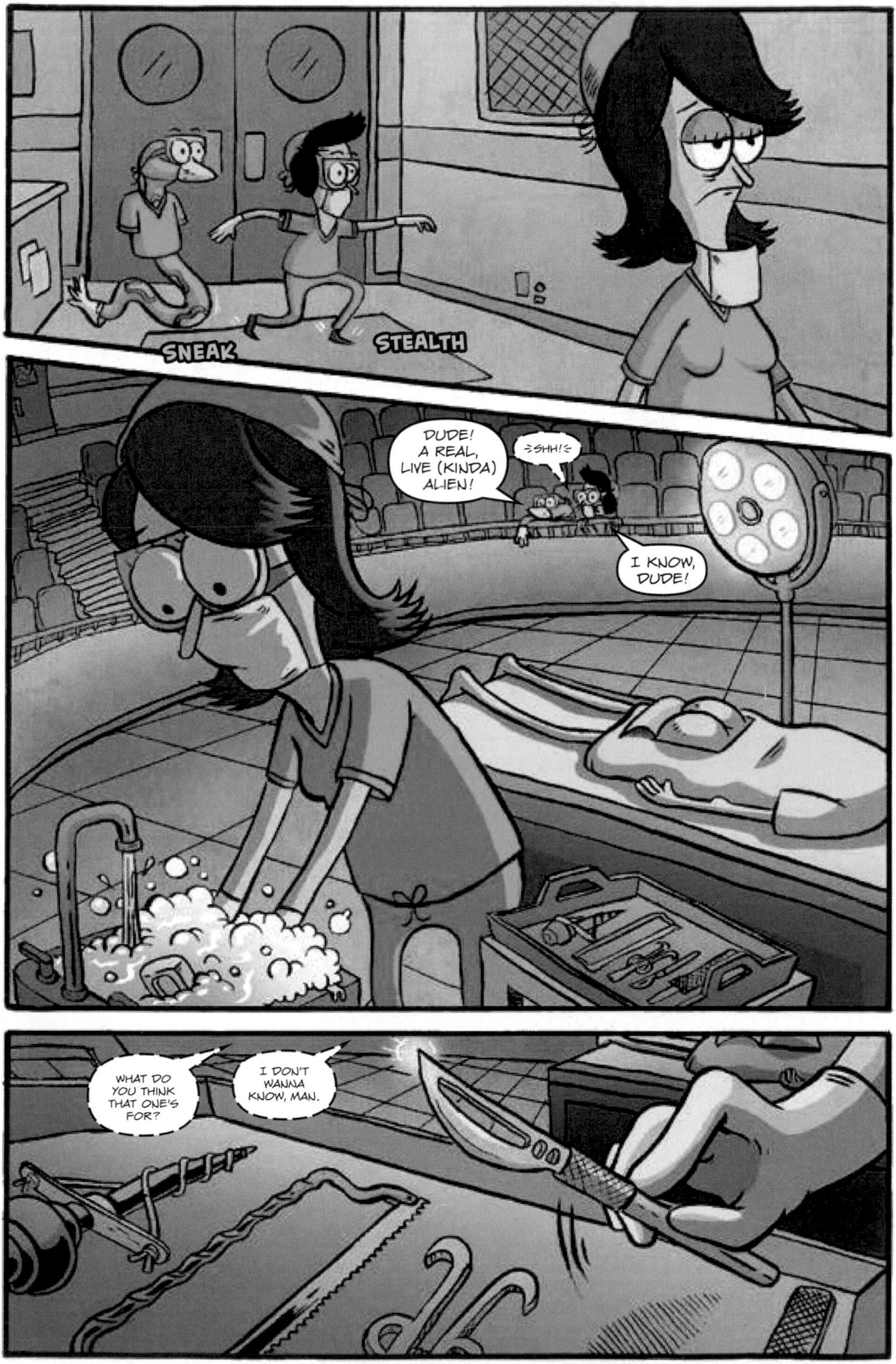
SNEAK
STEALTH
DUDE! A REAL, LIVE (KINDA) ALIEN!
SHH!
I KNOW, DUDE!
WHAT DO YOU THINK THAT ONE'S FOR?
I DON'T WANNA KNOW, MAN.

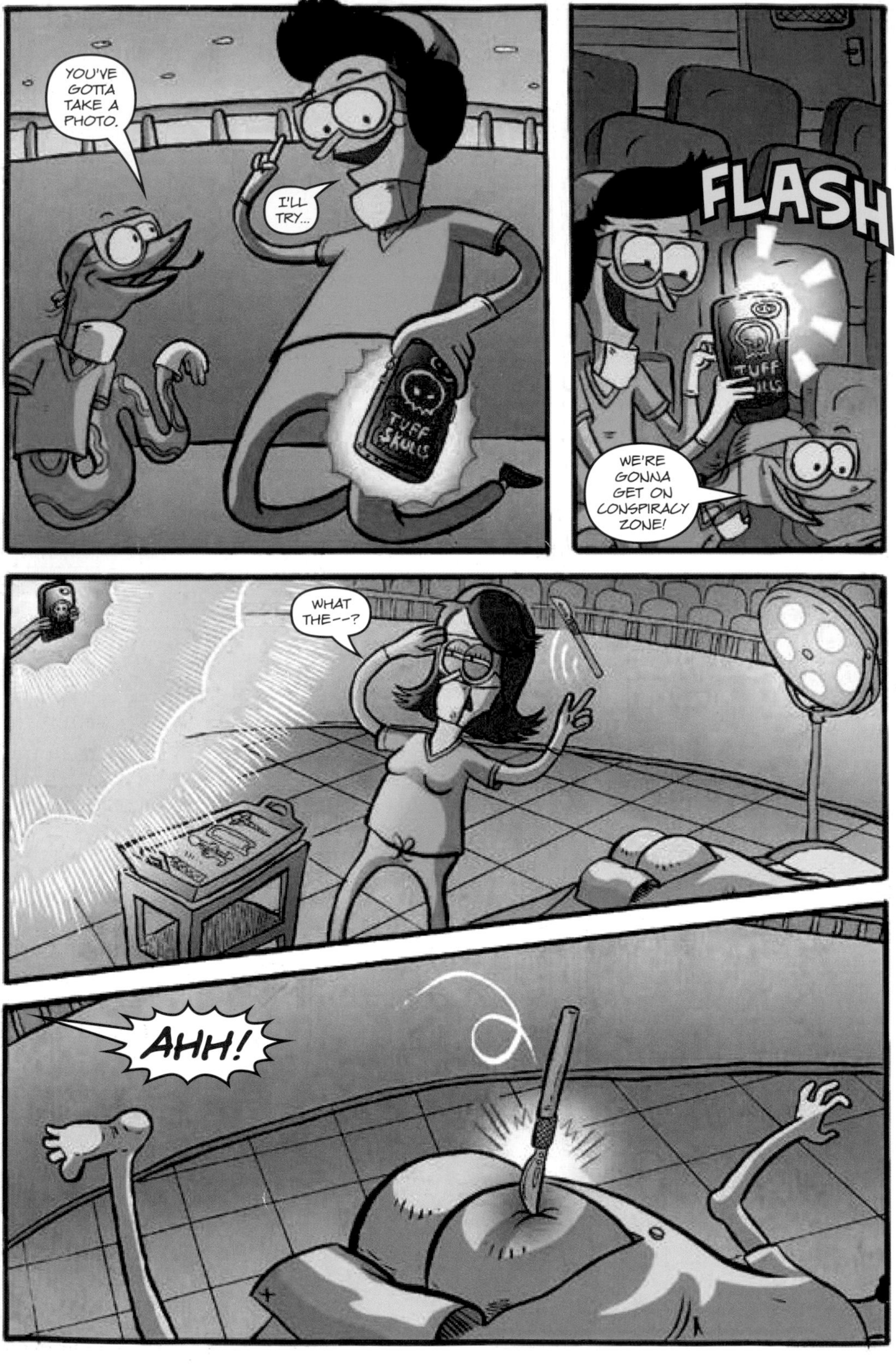
YOU'VE GOTTA TAKE A PHOTO.
I'LL TRY...
FLASH
WE'RE GONNA GET ON CONSPIRACY ZONE!
WHAT THE--?
AHH!

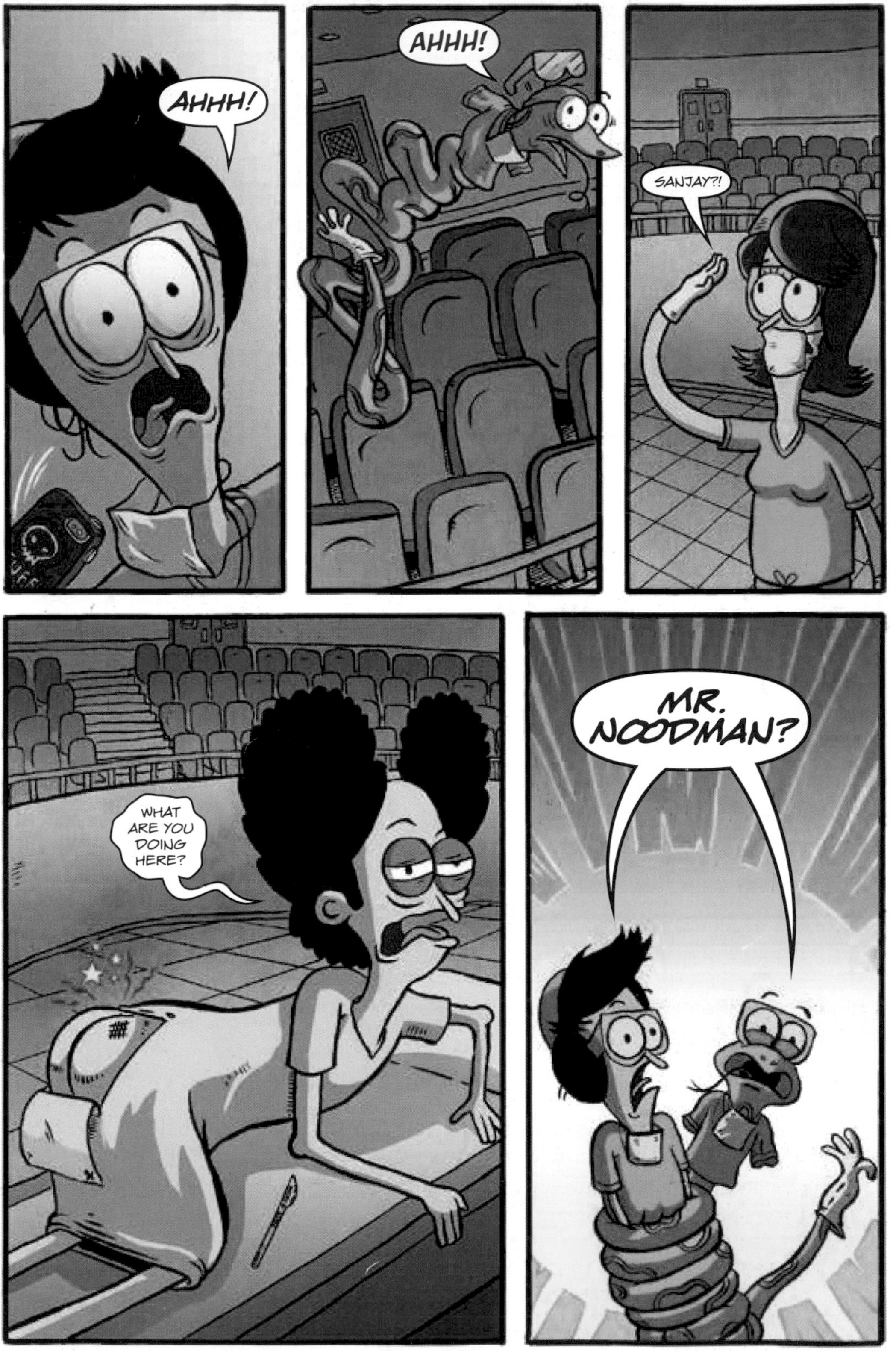
AHHH!
AHHH!
SANJAY?!
WHAT ARE YOU DOING HERE?
MR. NOODMAN?

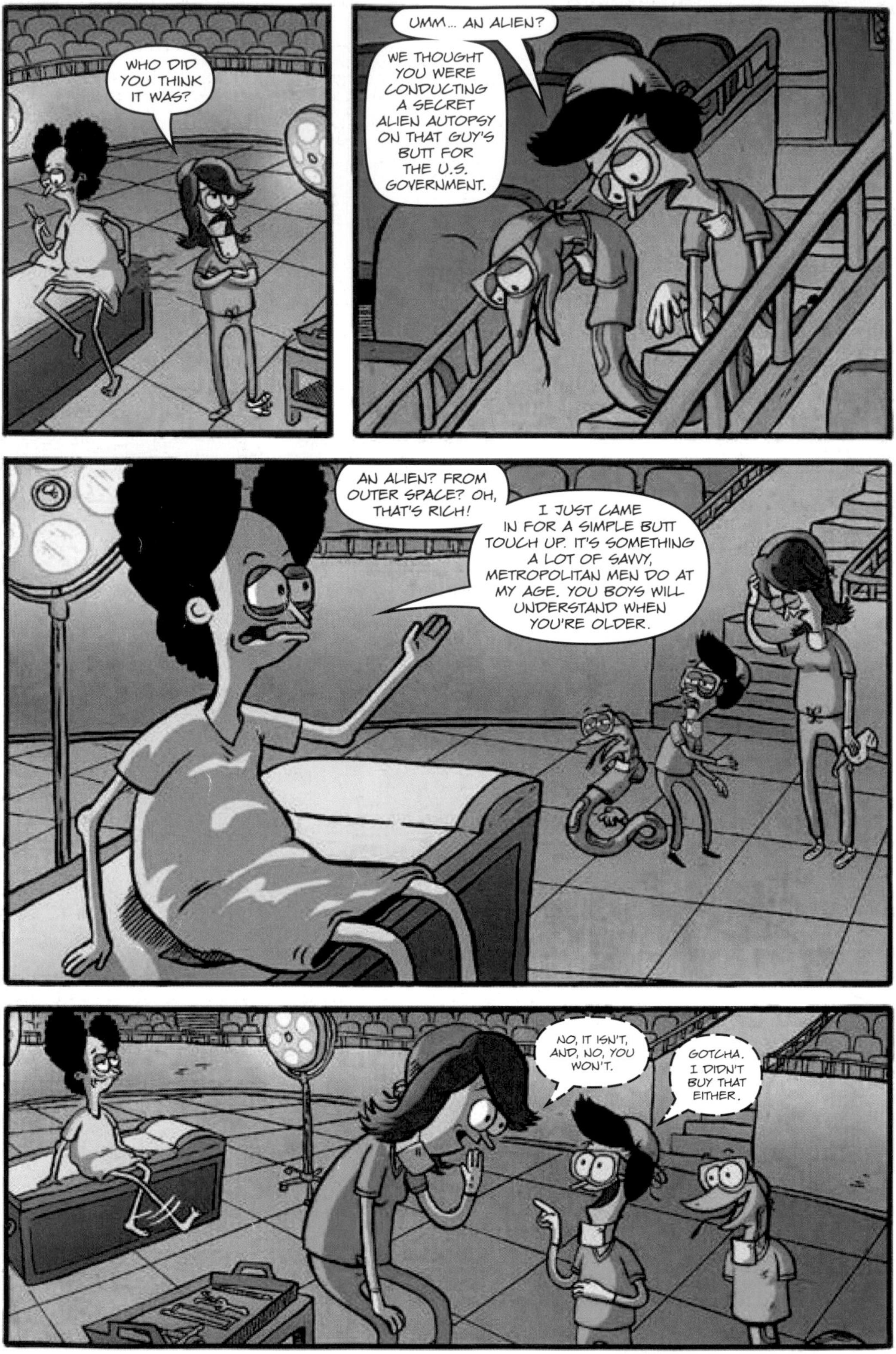
WHO DID YOU THINK IT WAS?
UMM... AN ALIEN?
WE THOUGHT YOU WERE CONDUCTING A SECRET ALIEN AUTOPSY ON THAT GUY'S BUTT FOR THE U.S. GOVERNMENT.
AN ALIEN? FROM OUTER SPACE? OH, THAT'S RICH!
I JUST CAME IN FOR A SIMPLE BUTT TOUCH UP. IT'S SOMETHING A LOT OF SAVVY, METROPOLITAN MEN DO AT MY AGE. YOU BOYS WILL UNDERSTAND WHEN YOU'RE OLDER.
NO, IT ISN'T, AND, NO, YOU WON'T.
GOTCHA. I DIDN'T BUY THAT EITHER.

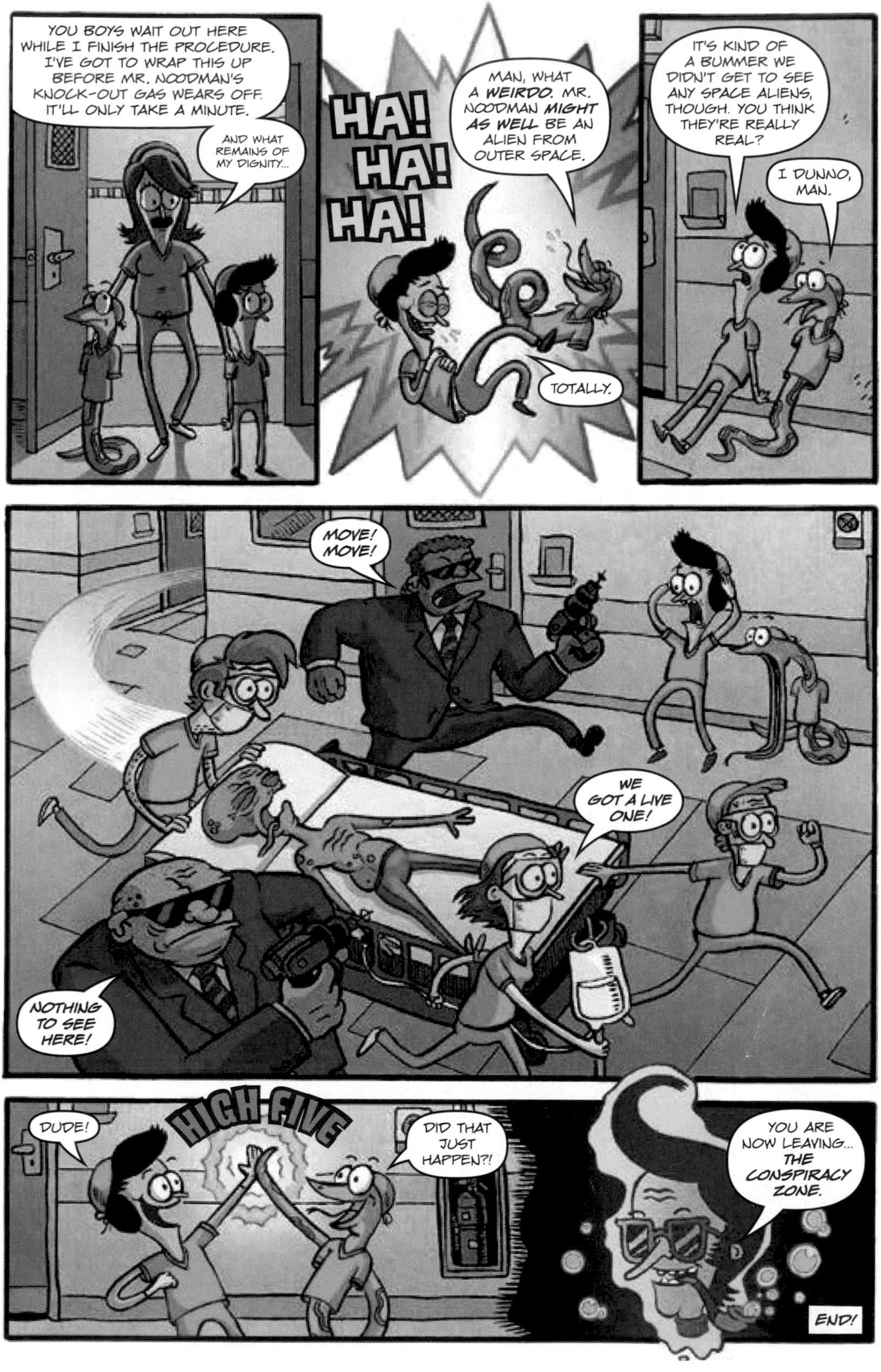
YOU BOYS WAIT OUT HERE WHILE I FINISH THE PROCEDURE. I'VE GOT TO WRAP THIS UP BEFORE MR. NOODMAN'S KNOCK-OUT GAS WEARS OFF. IT'LL ONLY TAKE A MINUTE.
AND WHAT REMAINS OF MY DIGNITY...
HA! HA! HA!
MAN, WHAT A WEIRDO. MR. NOODMAN MIGHT AS WELL BE AN ALIEN FROM OUTER SPACE.
TOTALLY.
IT'S KIND OF A BUMMER WE DIDN'T GET TO SEE ANY SPACE ALIENS, THOUGH. YOU THINK THEY'RE REALLY REAL?
I DUNNO, MAN.
MOVE! MOVE!
WE GOT A LIVE ONE!
NOTHING TO SEE HERE!
DUDE!
HIGH FIVE
DID THAT JUST HAPPEN?!
YOU ARE NOW LEAVING... THE CONSPIRACY ZONE.
END!

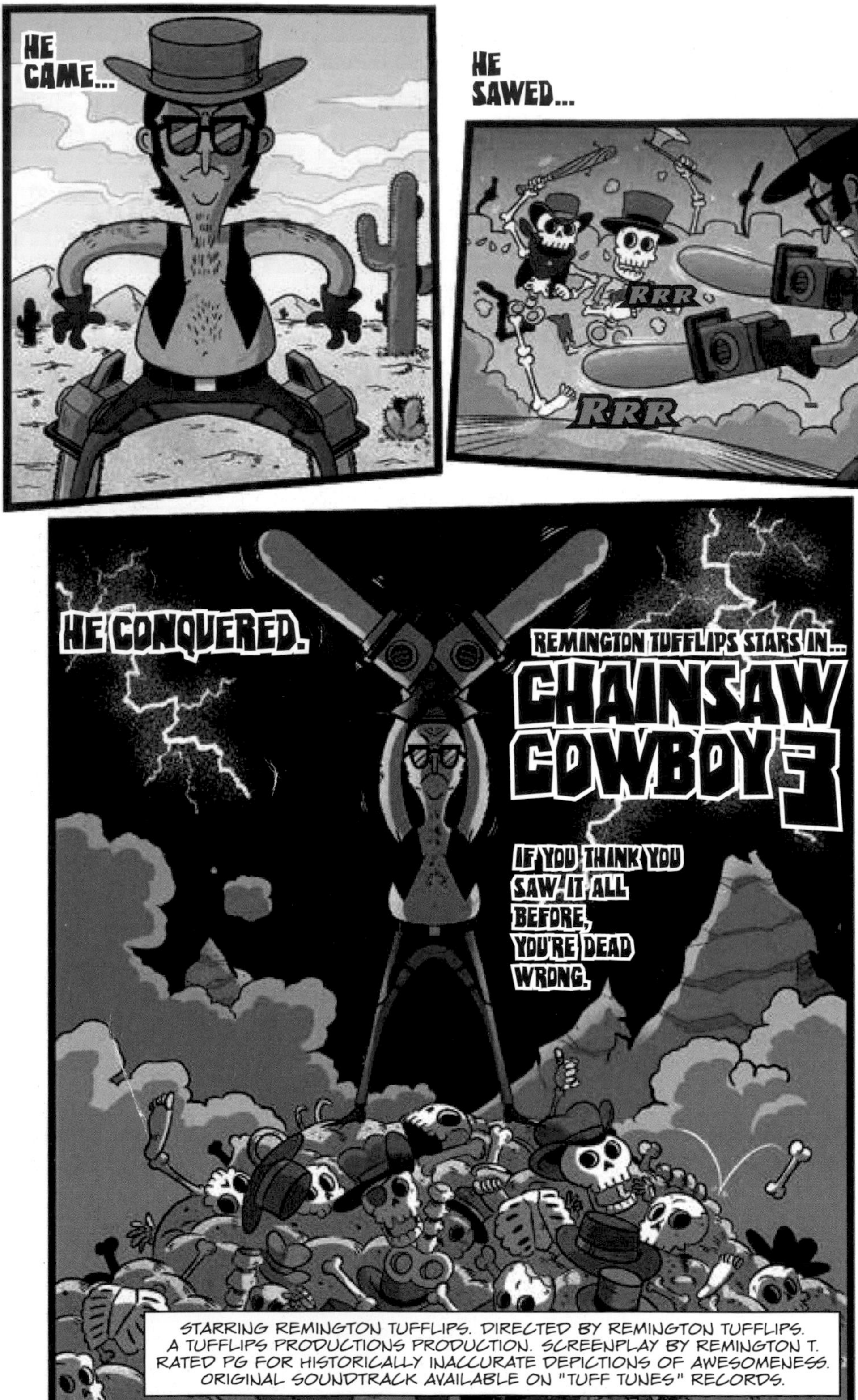
HE CAME...
HE SAWED...
RRR
RRR
HE CONQUERED.
REMINGTON TUFFLIPS STARS IN...
CHAINSAW COWBOY 3
IF YOU THINK YOU SAW IT ALL BEFORE, YOU'RE DEAD WRONG.
STARRING REMINGTON TUFFLIPS. DIRECTED BY REMINGTON TUFFLIPS.
A TUFFLIPS PRODUCTIONS PRODUCTION. SCREENPLAY BY REMINGTON T.
RATED PG FOR HISTORICALLY INACCURATE DEPICTIONS OF AWESOMENESS.
ORIGINAL SOUNDTRACK AVAILABLE ON "TUFF TUNES" RECORDS.

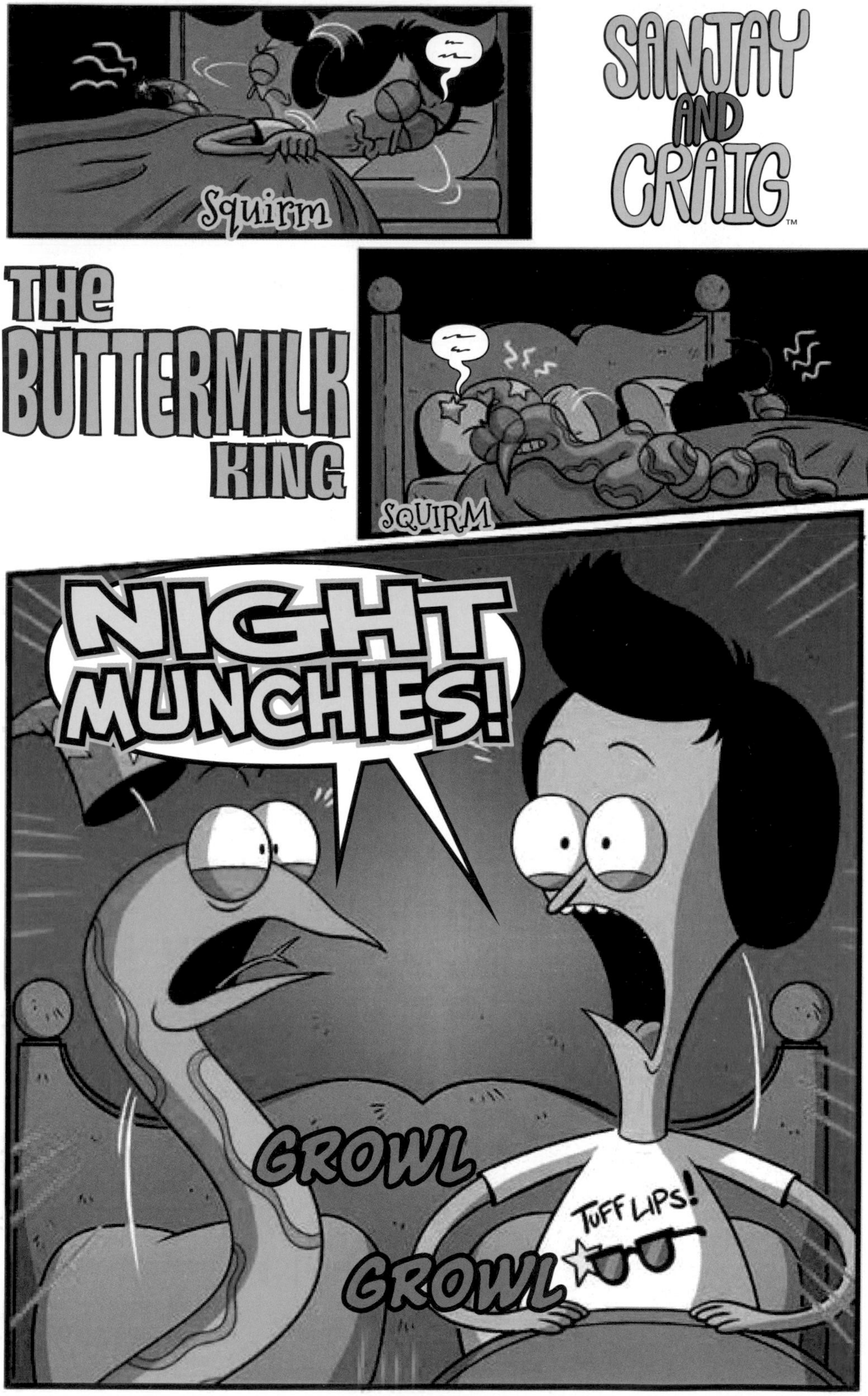
Squirm
SANJAY AND CRAIG™
THE BUTTERMILK KING
SQUIRM
NIGHT MUNCHIES!
GROWL
TUFF LIPS!
GROWL

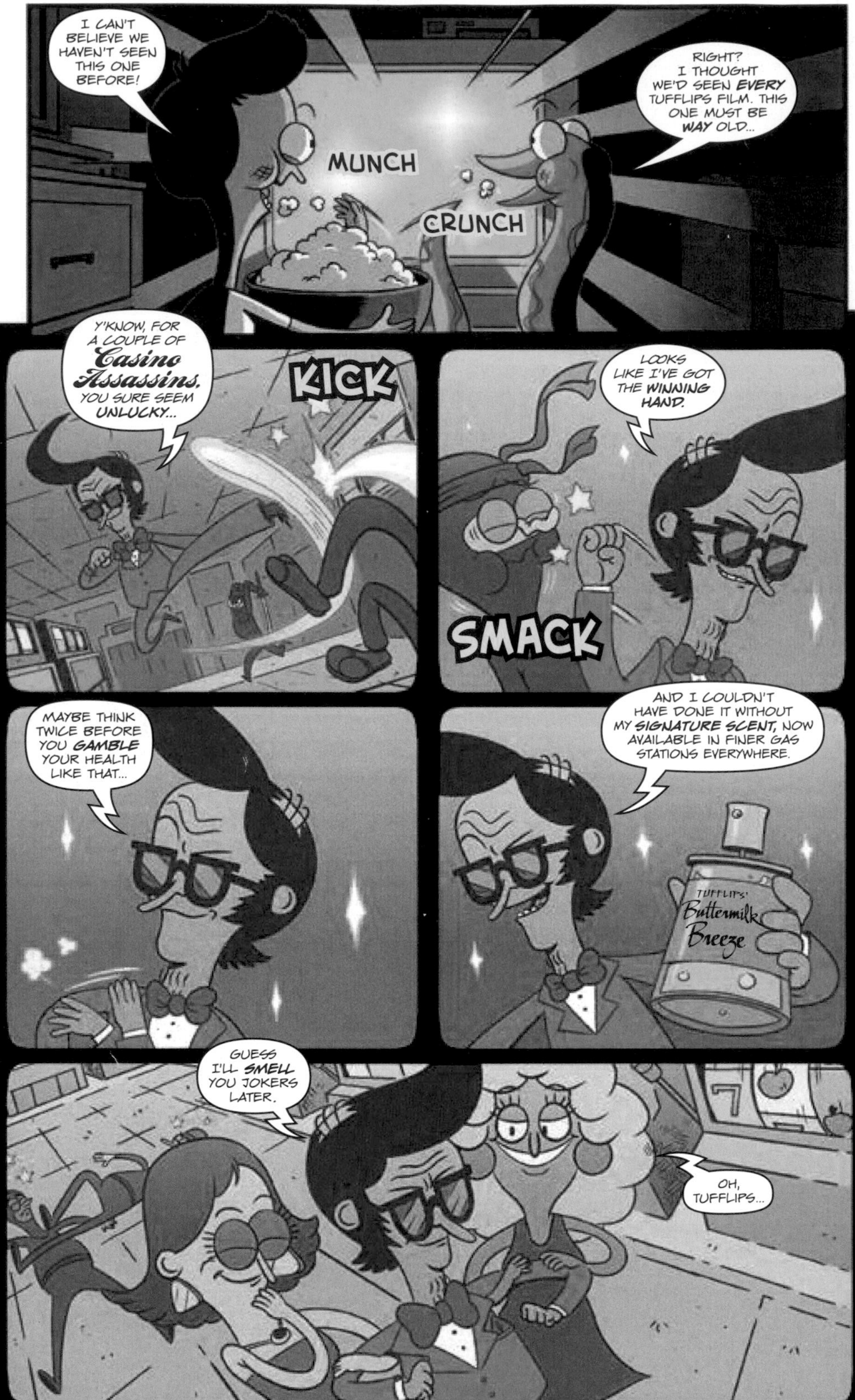
I CAN'T BELIEVE WE HAVEN'T SEEN THIS ONE BEFORE!
RIGHT? I THOUGHT WE'D SEEN EVERY TUFFLIPS FILM. THIS ONE MUST BE WAY OLD...
MUNCH
CRUNCH
Y'KNOW, FOR A COUPLE OF Casino Assassins, YOU SURE SEEM UNLUCKY...
KICK
LOOKS LIKE I'VE GOT THE WINNING HAND.
SMACK
MAYBE THINK TWICE BEFORE YOU GAMBLE YOUR HEALTH LIKE THAT...
AND I COULDN'T HAVE DONE IT WITHOUT MY SIGNATURE SCENT, NOW AVAILABLE IN FINER GAS STATIONS EVERYWHERE.
TUFFLIPS' Buttermilk Breeze
GUESS I'LL SMELL YOU JOKERS LATER.
OH, TUFFLIPS...

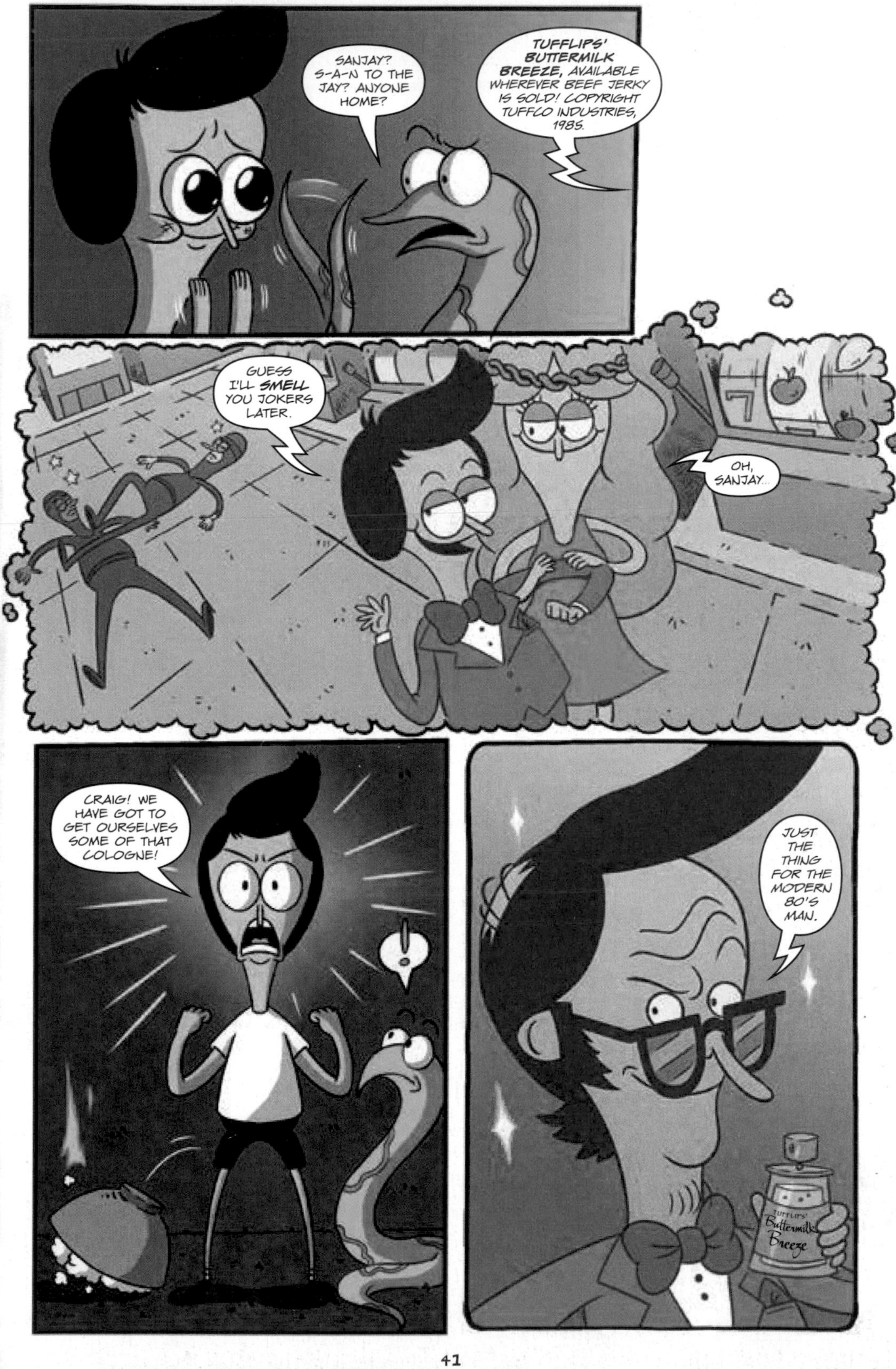
SANJAY? S-A-N TO THE JAY? ANYONE HOME?
TUFFLIPS' BUTTERMILK BREEZE, AVAILABLE WHEREVER BEEF JERKY IS SOLD! COPYRIGHT TUFFCO INDUSTRIES, 1985.
GUESS I'LL SMELL YOU JOKERS LATER.
OH, SANJAY...
CRAIG! WE HAVE GOT TO GET OURSELVES SOME OF THAT COLOGNE!
JUST THE THING FOR THE MODERN 80'S MAN.
TUFFLIPS' Buttermilk Breeze

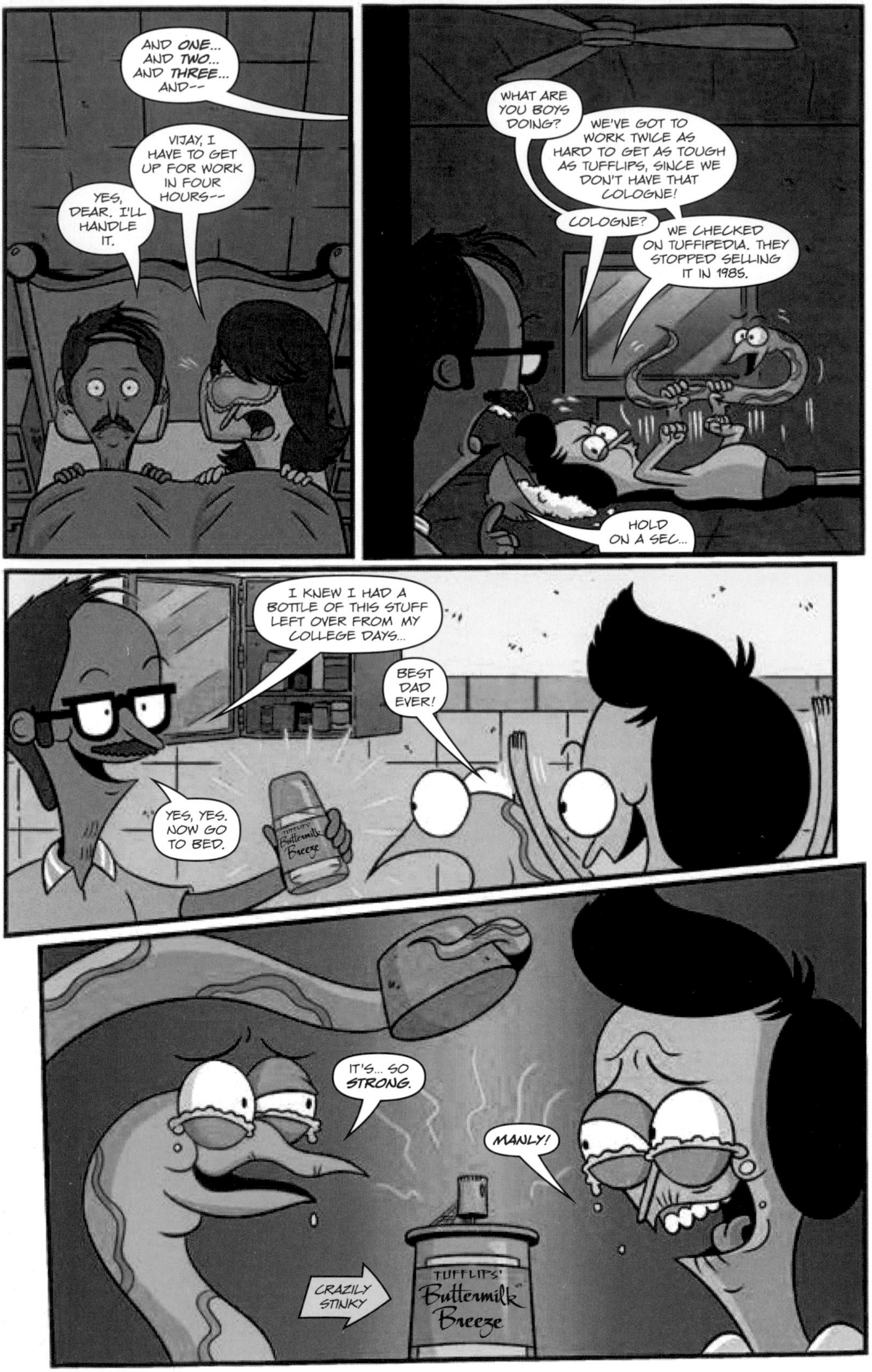
AND ONE... AND TWO... AND THREE... AND--
VIJAY, I HAVE TO GET UP FOR WORK IN FOUR HOURS--
YES, DEAR. I'LL HANDLE IT.
WHAT ARE YOU BOYS DOING?
WE'VE GOT TO WORK TWICE AS HARD TO GET AS TOUGH AS TUFFLIPS, SINCE WE DON'T HAVE THAT COLOGNE!
COLOGNE?
WE CHECKED ON TUFFIPEDIA. THEY STOPPED SELLING IT IN 1985.
HOLD ON A SEC...
I KNEW I HAD A BOTTLE OF THIS STUFF LEFT OVER FROM MY COLLEGE DAYS...
BEST DAD EVER!
YES, YES. NOW GO TO BED.
TUFFLIPS' Buttermilk Breeze
IT'S... SO STRONG.
MANLY!
CRAZILY STINKY
TUFFLIPS' Buttermilk Breeze

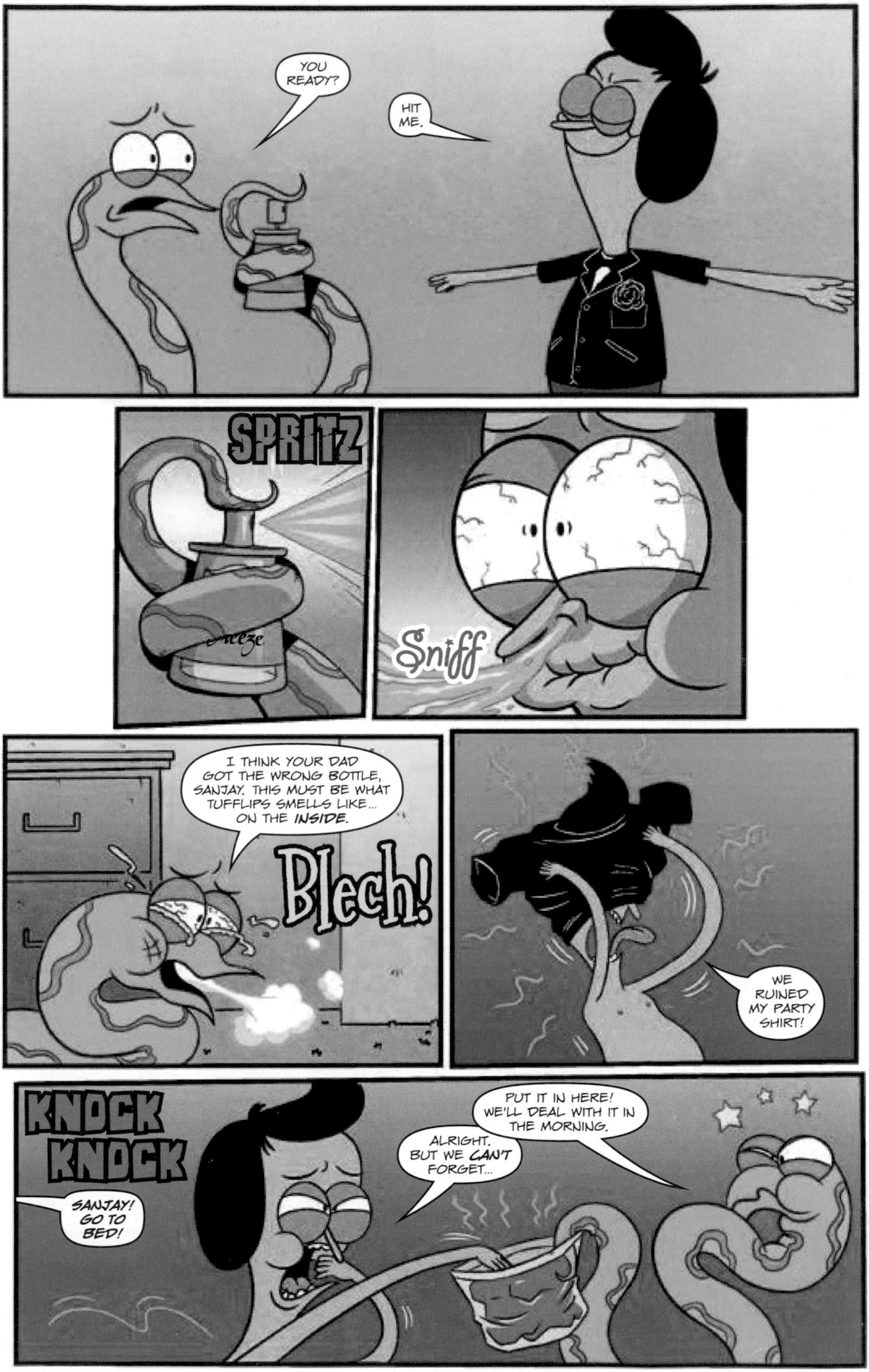
YOU READY?
HIT ME.
SPRITZ
Sniff
I THINK YOUR DAD GOT THE WRONG BOTTLE, SANJAY. THIS MUST BE WHAT TUFFLIPS SMELLS LIKE... ON THE INSIDE.
Blech!
WE RUINED MY PARTY SHIRT!
KNOCK KNOCK
SANJAY! GO TO BED!
ALRIGHT. BUT WE CAN'T FORGET...
PUT IT IN HERE! WE'LL DEAL WITH IT IN THE MORNING.

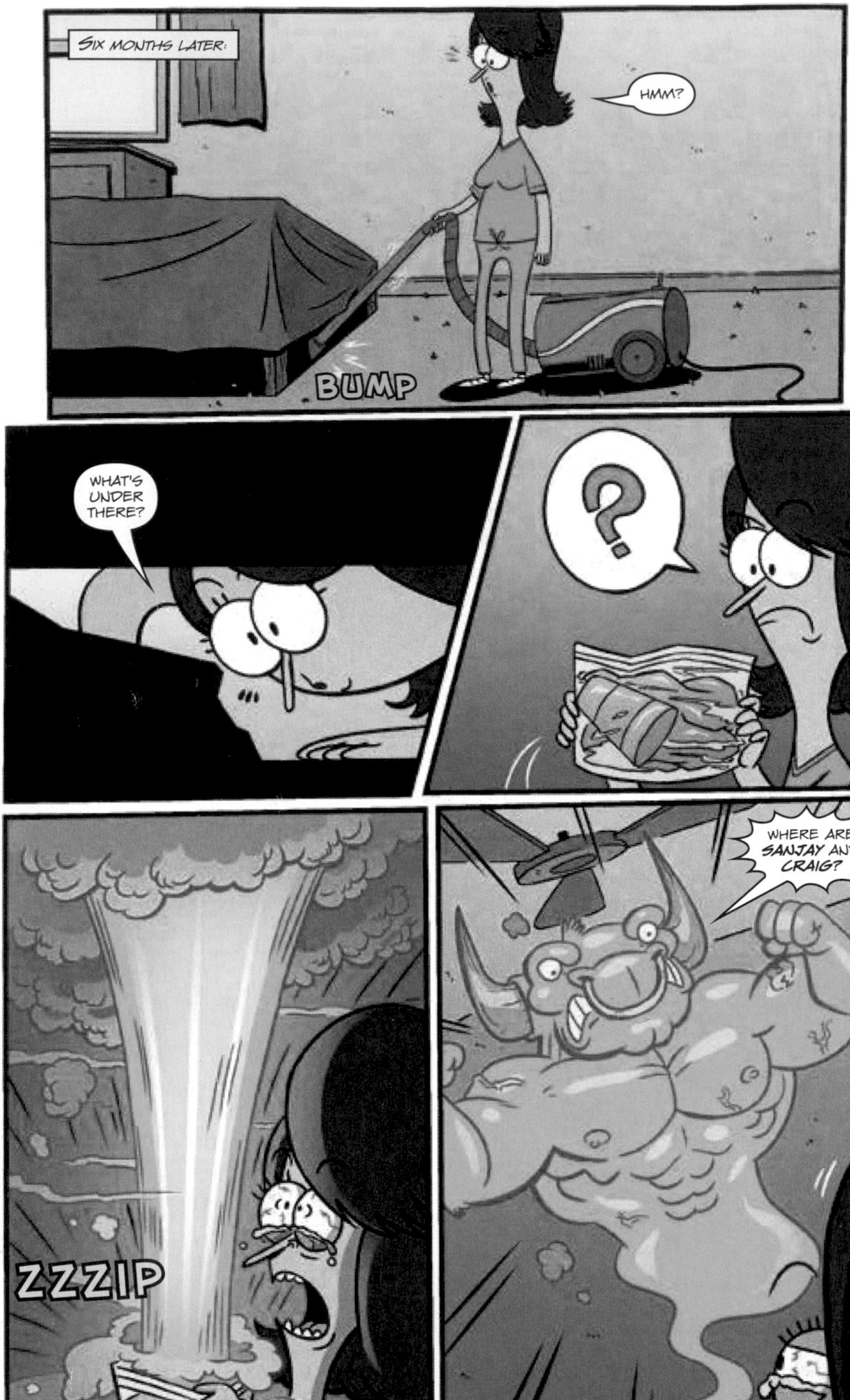

SIX MONTHS LATER:
HMM?
BUMP
WHAT'S UNDER THERE?
?
ZZZIP
WHERE ARE SANJAY AND CRAIG?

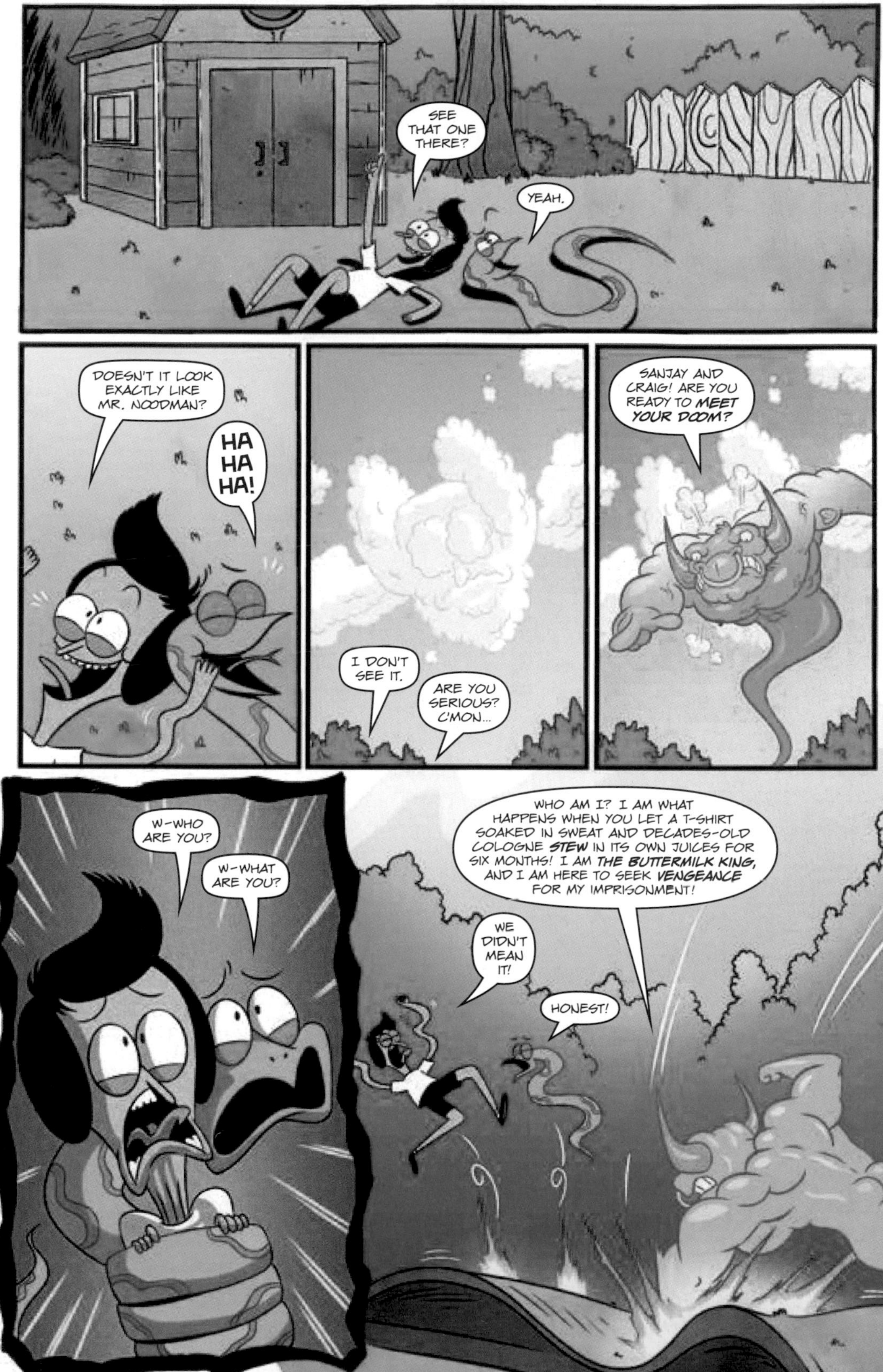
SEE THAT ONE THERE?
YEAH.
DOESN'T IT LOOK EXACTLY LIKE MR. NOODMAN?
HA HA HA!
I DON'T SEE IT.
ARE YOU SERIOUS? C'MON...
SANJAY AND CRAIG! ARE YOU READY TO MEET YOUR DOOM?
W-WHO ARE YOU?
W-WHAT ARE YOU?
WHO AM I? I AM WHAT HAPPENS WHEN YOU LET A T-SHIRT SOAKED IN SWEAT AND DECADES-OLD COLOGNE STEW IN ITS OWN JUICES FOR SIX MONTHS! I AM THE BUTTERMILK KING, AND I AM HERE TO SEEK VENGEANCE FOR MY IMPRISONMENT!
WE DIDN'T MEAN IT!
HONEST!

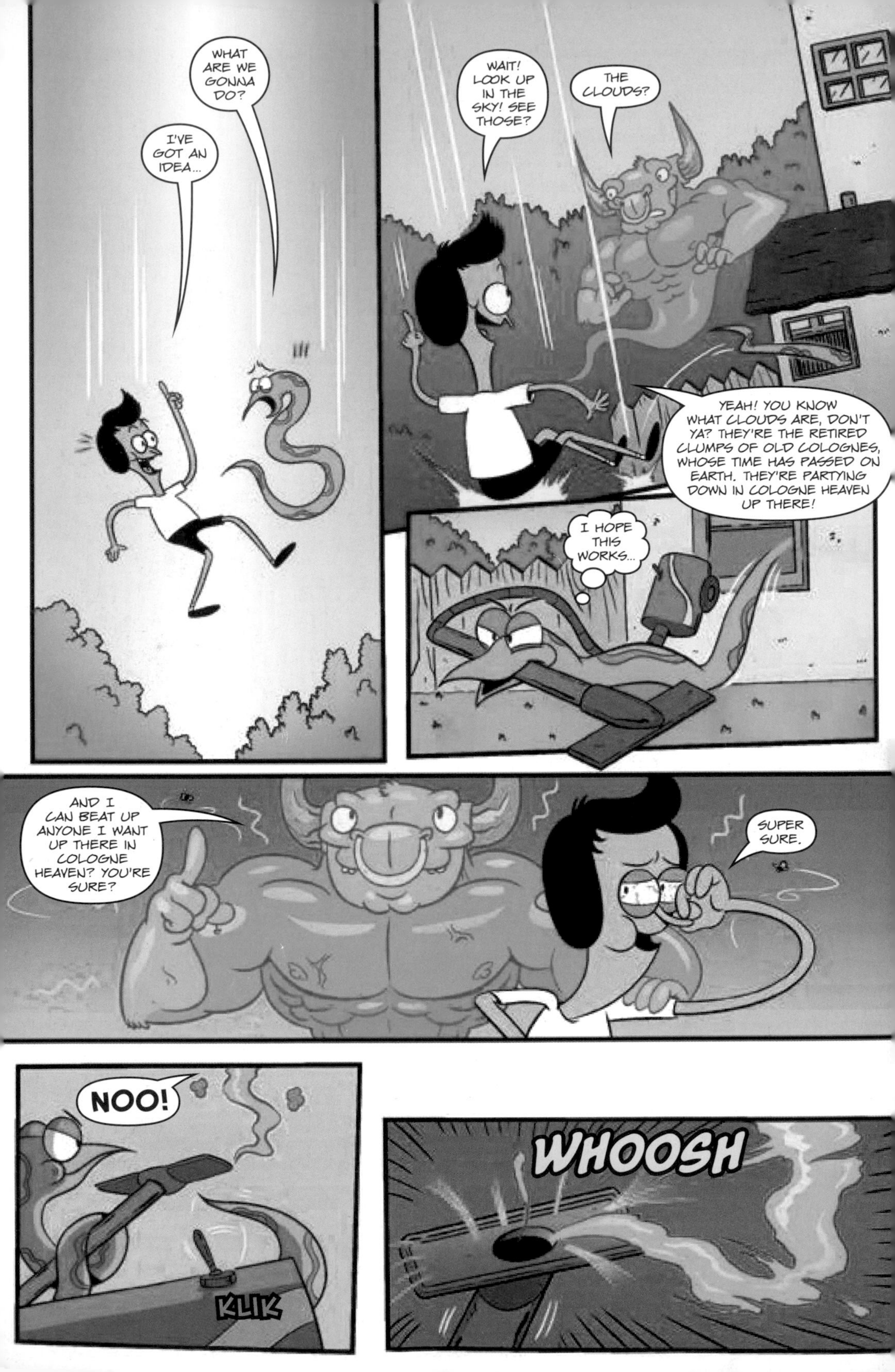
WHAT ARE WE GONNA DO?
I'VE GOT AN IDEA...
WAIT! LOOK UP IN THE SKY! SEE THOSE?
THE CLOUDS?
YEAH! YOU KNOW WHAT CLOUDS ARE, DON'T YA? THEY'RE THE RETIRED CLUMPS OF OLD COLOGNES, WHOSE TIME HAS PASSED ON EARTH. THEY'RE PARTYING DOWN IN COLOGNE HEAVEN UP THERE!
I HOPE THIS WORKS...
AND I CAN BEAT UP ANYONE I WANT UP THERE IN COLOGNE HEAVEN? YOU'RE SURE?
SUPER SURE.
NOO!
KLIK
WHOOSH

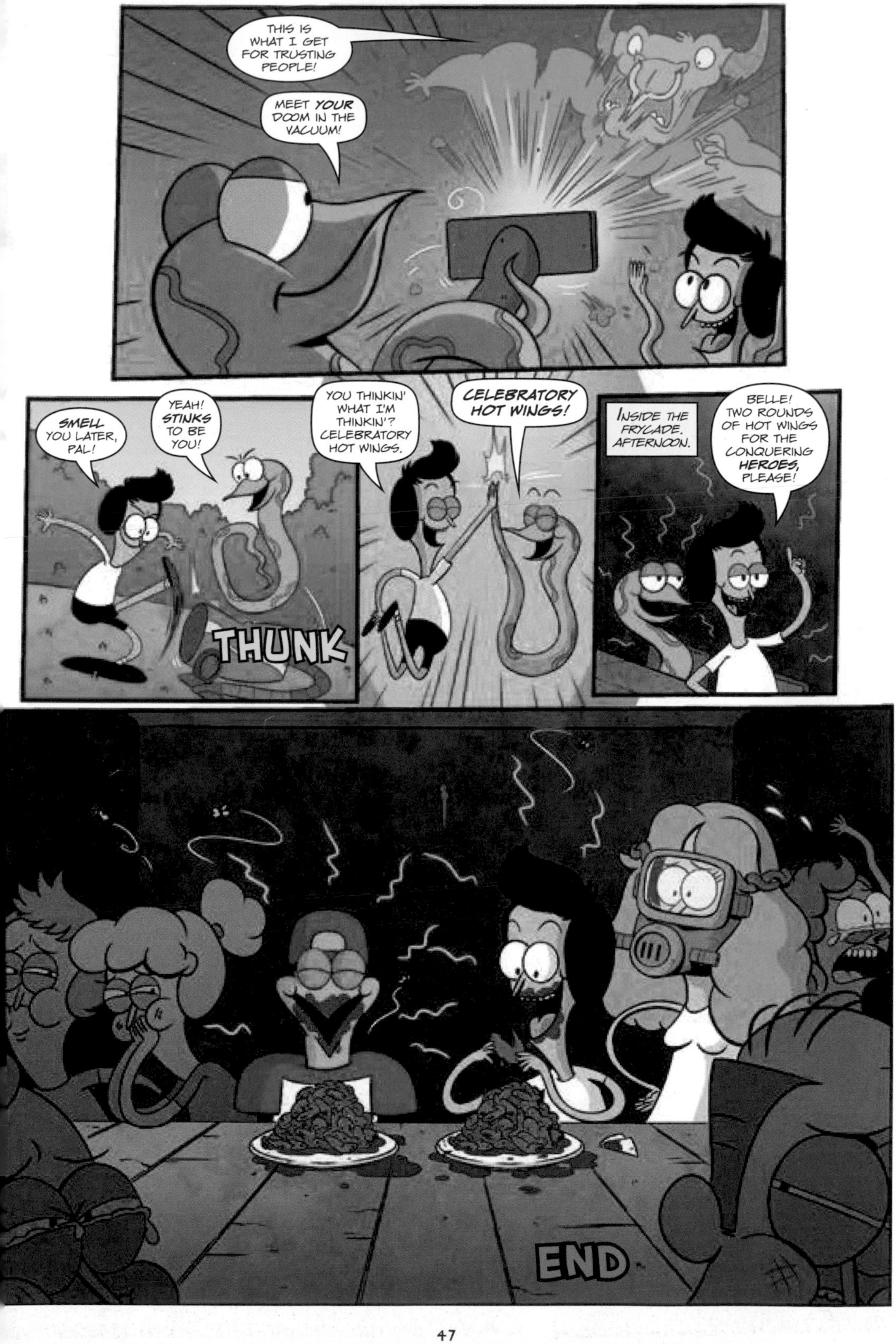

THIS IS WHAT I GET FOR TRUSTING PEOPLE!
MEET YOUR DOOM IN THE VACUUM!
SMELL YOU LATER, PAL!
YEAH! STINKS TO BE YOU!
THUNK
YOU THINKIN' WHAT I'M THINKIN'? CELEBRATORY HOT WINGS.
CELEBRATORY HOT WINGS!
INSIDE THE FRYCADE. AFTERNOON.
BELLE! TWO ROUNDS OF HOT WINGS FOR THE CONQUERING HEROES, PLEASE!
END

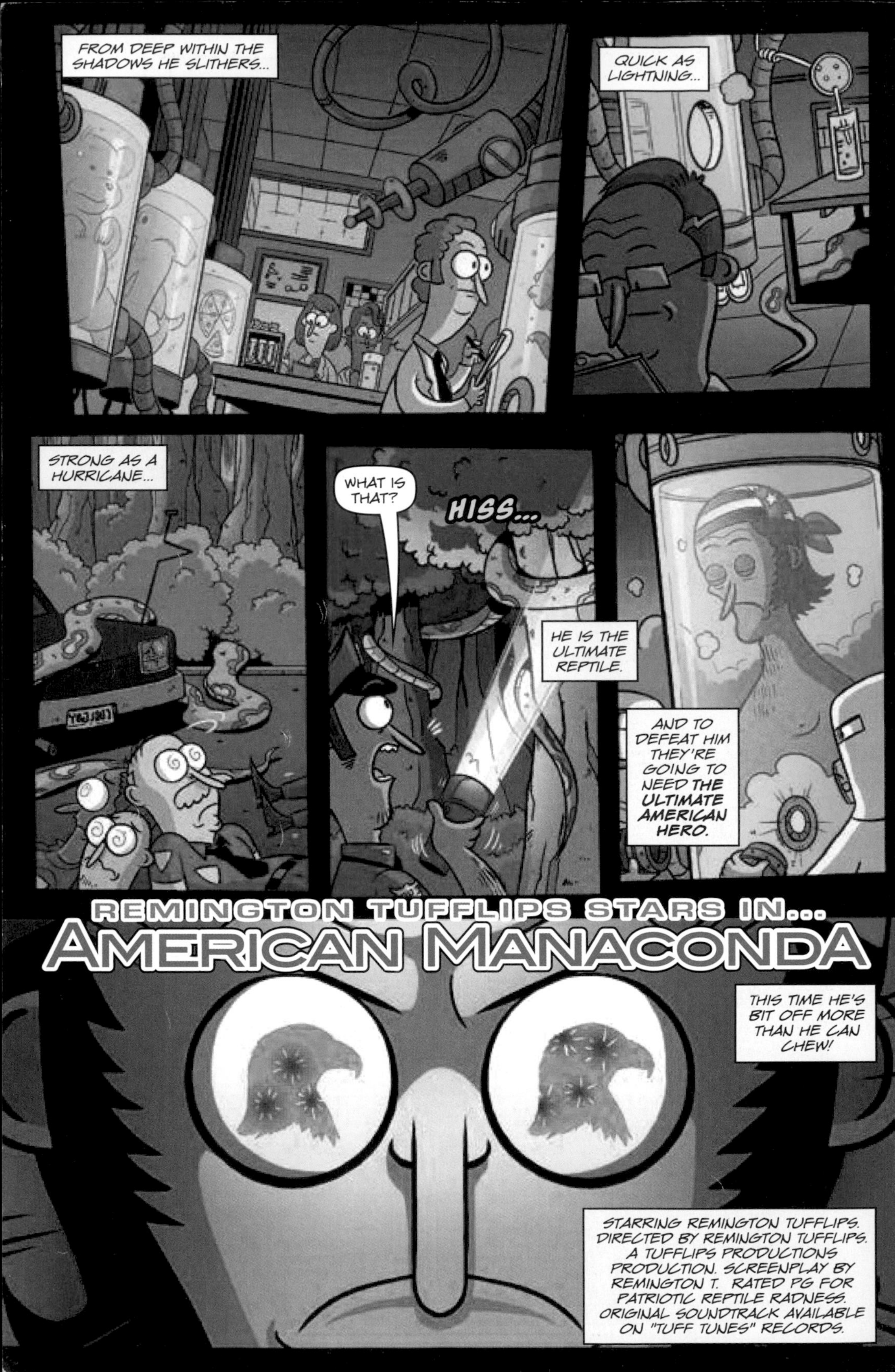
FROM DEEP WITHIN THE SHADOWS HE SLITHERS...
QUICK AS LIGHTNING...
STRONG AS A HURRICANE...
WHAT IS THAT?
HISS...
HE IS THE ULTIMATE REPTILE.
AND TO DEFEAT HIM THEY'RE GOING TO NEED THE ULTIMATE AMERICAN HERO.
REMINGTON TUFFLIPS STARS IN...
AMERICAN MANACONDA
THIS TIME HE'S BIT OFF MORE THAN HE CAN CHEW!
STARRING REMINGTON TUFFLIPS. DIRECTED BY REMINGTON TUFFLIPS. A TUFFLIPS PRODUCTIONS PRODUCTION. SCREENPLAY BY REMINGTON T. RATED PG FOR PATRIOTIC REPTILE RADNESS. ORIGINAL SOUNDTRACK AVAILABLE ON "TUFF TUNES" RECORDS.

WATCH OUT FOR PAPERCUTZ

Welcome to the fiery-flavored first SANJAY AND CRAIG graphic novel from Papercutz—those hot-wing lovin', video game-playin' people who are dedicated to publishing great graphic novels for all ages. I'm Jim Salicrup, the enthusiastic Editor-in-Chief, and I'm here to take you behind-the-scenes and offer a peek at what we have planned for you in the future!

But let's start at the beginning. A little over ten years ago, Papercutz publisher Terry Nantier and I founded this little comicbook company to address a need—there just didn't seem to be enough comics and graphic novels for kids. That was incredibly ironic, since most folks think of comics as being for kids. After ten years of producing all types of comics for all ages, we made an incredible deal with the awesome folks at Nickelodeon to create a line of graphic novels based on their latest and greatest new animated series. This really is a match made in cartoon heaven – Nickelodeon, loved by millions of kids for their brilliant cartoon shows and characters, and Papercutz, the graphic novel publisher devoted to creating the best comics for kids—together at last!

Terry and I, along with Joan Hilty and Linda Lee, got to spend a day at the Nickelodeon Animation Studio where we talked about our plans with the creators of Sanjay and Craig, Breadwinners, and more. Everyone was excited and as thrilled as we were about the characters leaping off the TV screen and onto the comicbook page!

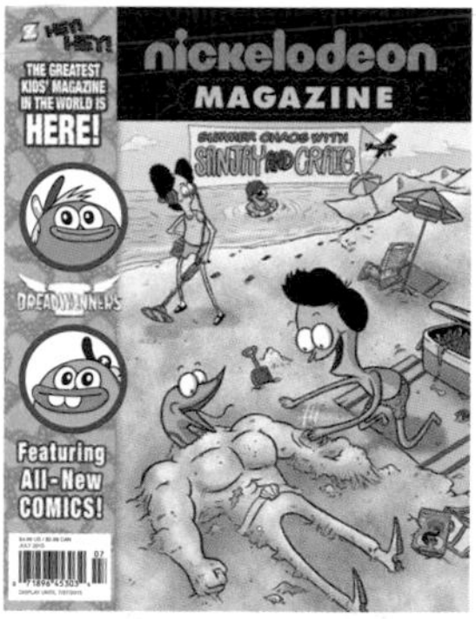
HEY! HEY!
THE GREATEST KIDS' MAGAZINE IN THE WORLD IS HERE!
nickelodeon
MAGAZINE
SUMMER CHAOS WITH SANJAY AND CRAIG
BREADWINNERS
Featuring All-New COMICS!

To kick off this historic publishing partnership, we launched an all-new NICKELODEON MAGAZINE, which in addition to features such as posters, activities, calendars, etc., is jam-packed with comics—the very same comics we'll be collecting in our graphic novels. The magazine is available wherever magazines are sold, and is also available as a subscription. Just go to Papercutz.com/nickmag for all the details.

Editors Michael Petranek and Suzannah Rowntree helped get the comics started, but the bulk of the editorial work was handled by Bethany Bryan (Associate Editor/Papercutz) and Joan Hilty (Comics Editor/Nickelodeon). Together, working with writer Eric Esquivel, and artists Sam Spina, James Kaminski, and Ryan Jampole, colorist Laurie E. Smith, and letterer Tom Orzechowski they've come up with the SANJAY AND CRAIG graphic novel you see before you.

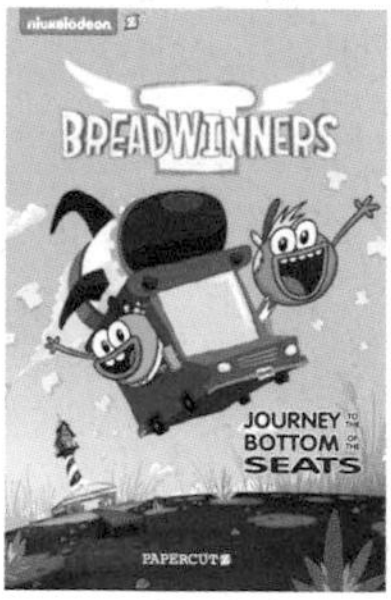
nickelodeon
BREADWINNERS
JOURNEY
BOTTOM
SEATS
PAPERCUTZ

But this is just the beginning! Coming up next will be the premiere BREADWINNERS graphic novel, followed by the first HARVEY BEAKS graphic novel, and then that's quickly followed by the debut of the first PIG GOAT BANANA CRICKET graphic novel! Is this the Nickelodeon Age of graphic novels or what? And the best part is that you are a BIG part of it! Tell us what you think of what we're doing—your opinion matters to us. Our goal is to produce graphic novels that you will love as much as the original TV shows. Write to us at the addresses below and tell us if we succeeded or not. We'll be waiting for your comments!

Thanks,

Jim

STAY IN TOUCH!

EMAIL:	salicrup@papercutz.com
WEB:	papercutz.com
TWITTER:	@papercutzgn
FACEBOOK:	PAPERCUTZGRAPHICNOVELS
FANMAIL:	Papercutz, 160 Broadway, Suite 700, East Wing, New York, NY 10038

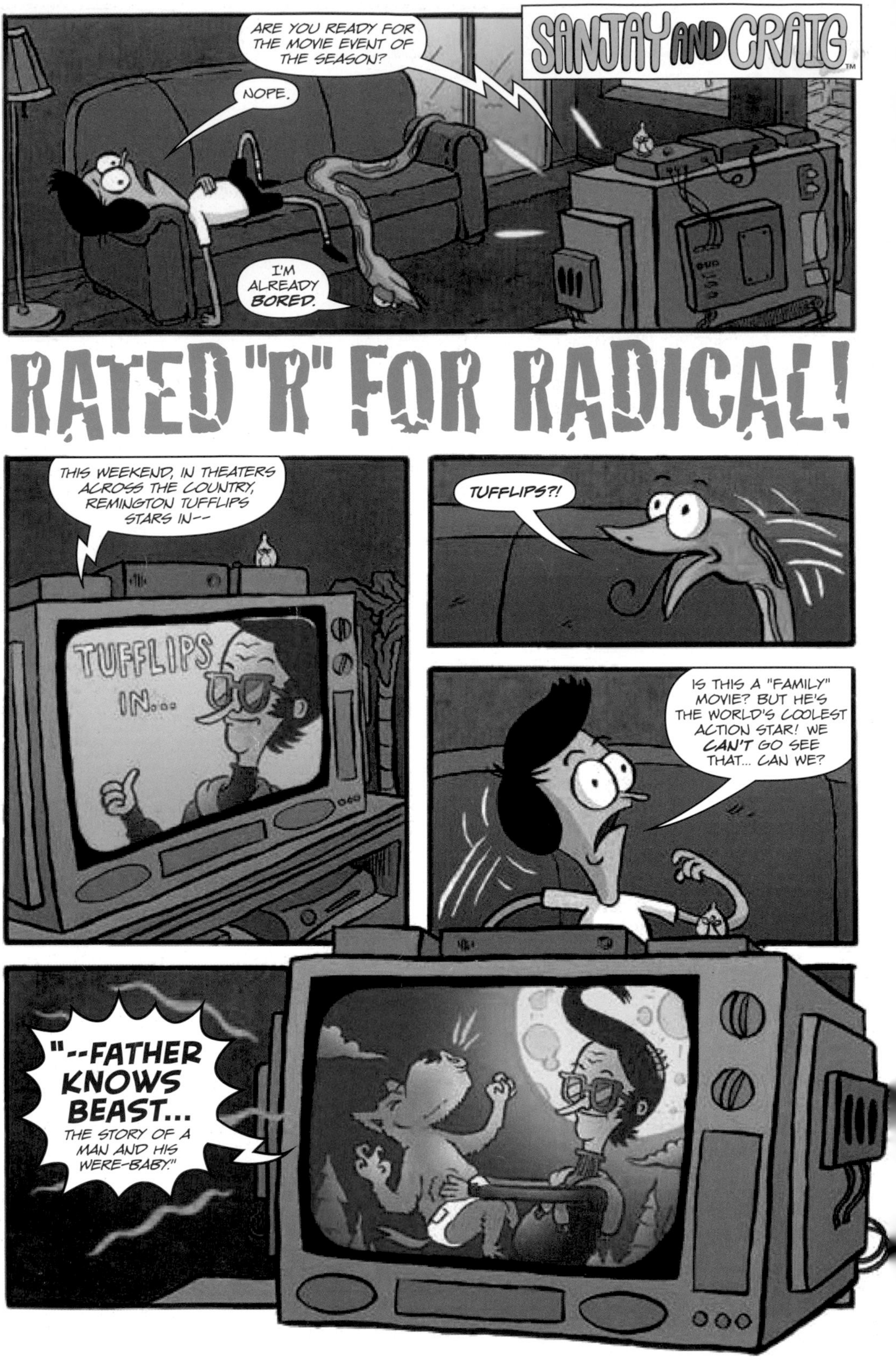
SANJAY AND CRAIG™
ARE YOU READY FOR THE MOVIE EVENT OF THE SEASON?
NOPE.
I'M ALREADY BORED.
RATED "R" FOR RADICAL!
THIS WEEKEND, IN THEATERS ACROSS THE COUNTRY, REMINGTON TUFFLIPS STARS IN--
TUFFLIPS IN...
TUFFLIPS?!
IS THIS A "FAMILY" MOVIE? BUT HE'S THE WORLD'S COOLEST ACTION STAR! WE CAN'T GO SEE THAT... CAN WE?
"--FATHER KNOWS BEAST... THE STORY OF A MAN AND HIS WERE-BABY."

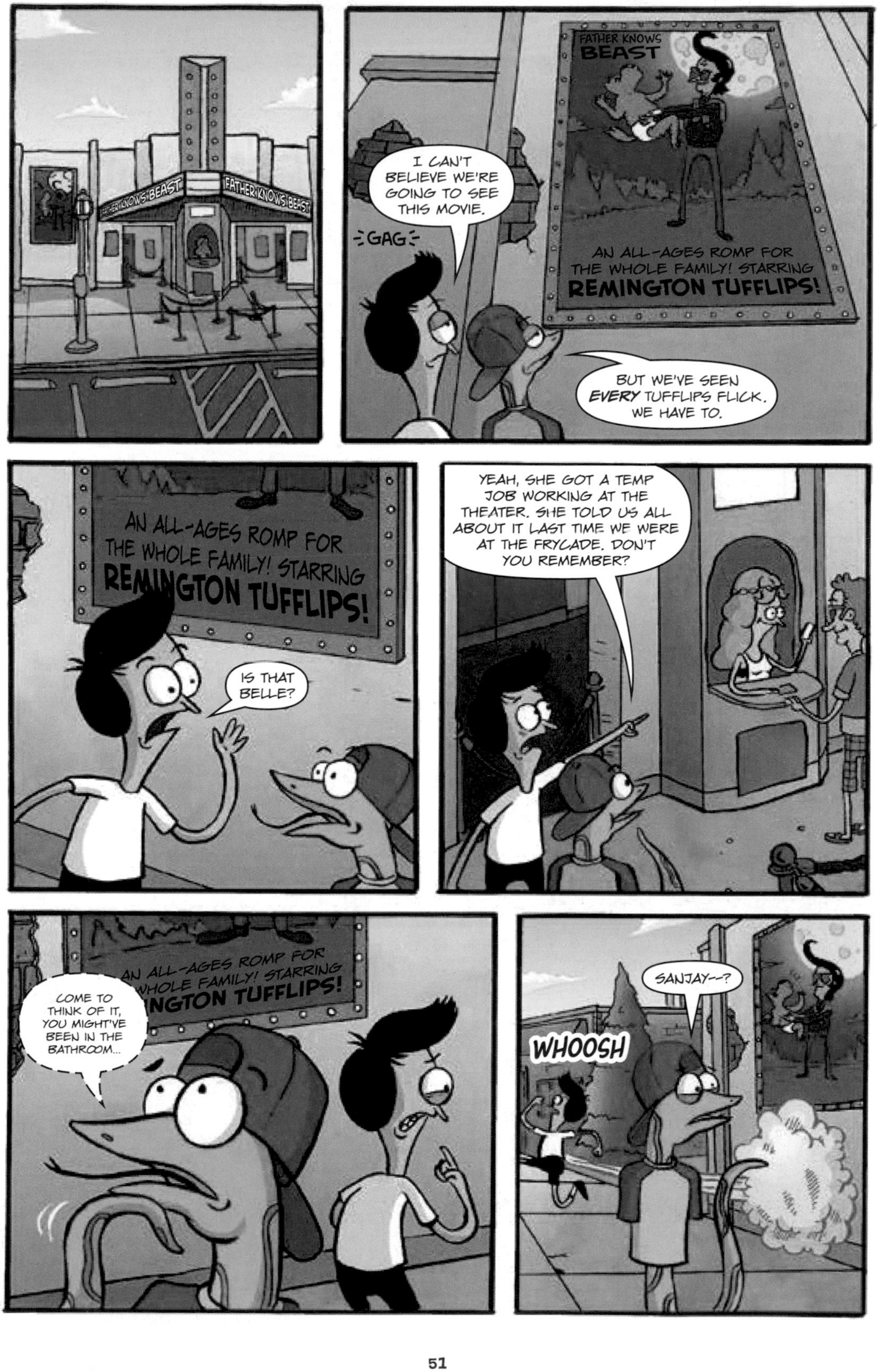
FATHER KNOWS BEAST
FATHER KNOWS BEAST
FATHER KNOWS BEAST
I CAN'T BELIEVE WE'RE GOING TO SEE THIS MOVIE.
GAG
AN ALL-AGES ROMP FOR THE WHOLE FAMILY! STARRING REMINGTON TUFFLIPS!
BUT WE'VE SEEN *EVERY* TUFFLIPS FLICK. WE HAVE TO.
AN ALL-AGES ROMP FOR THE WHOLE FAMILY! STARRING REMINGTON TUFFLIPS!
IS THAT BELLE?
YEAH, SHE GOT A TEMP JOB WORKING AT THE THEATER. SHE TOLD US ALL ABOUT IT LAST TIME WE WERE AT THE FRYCADE. DON'T YOU REMEMBER?
COME TO THINK OF IT, YOU MIGHT'VE BEEN IN THE BATHROOM...
SANJAY--?
WHOOSH

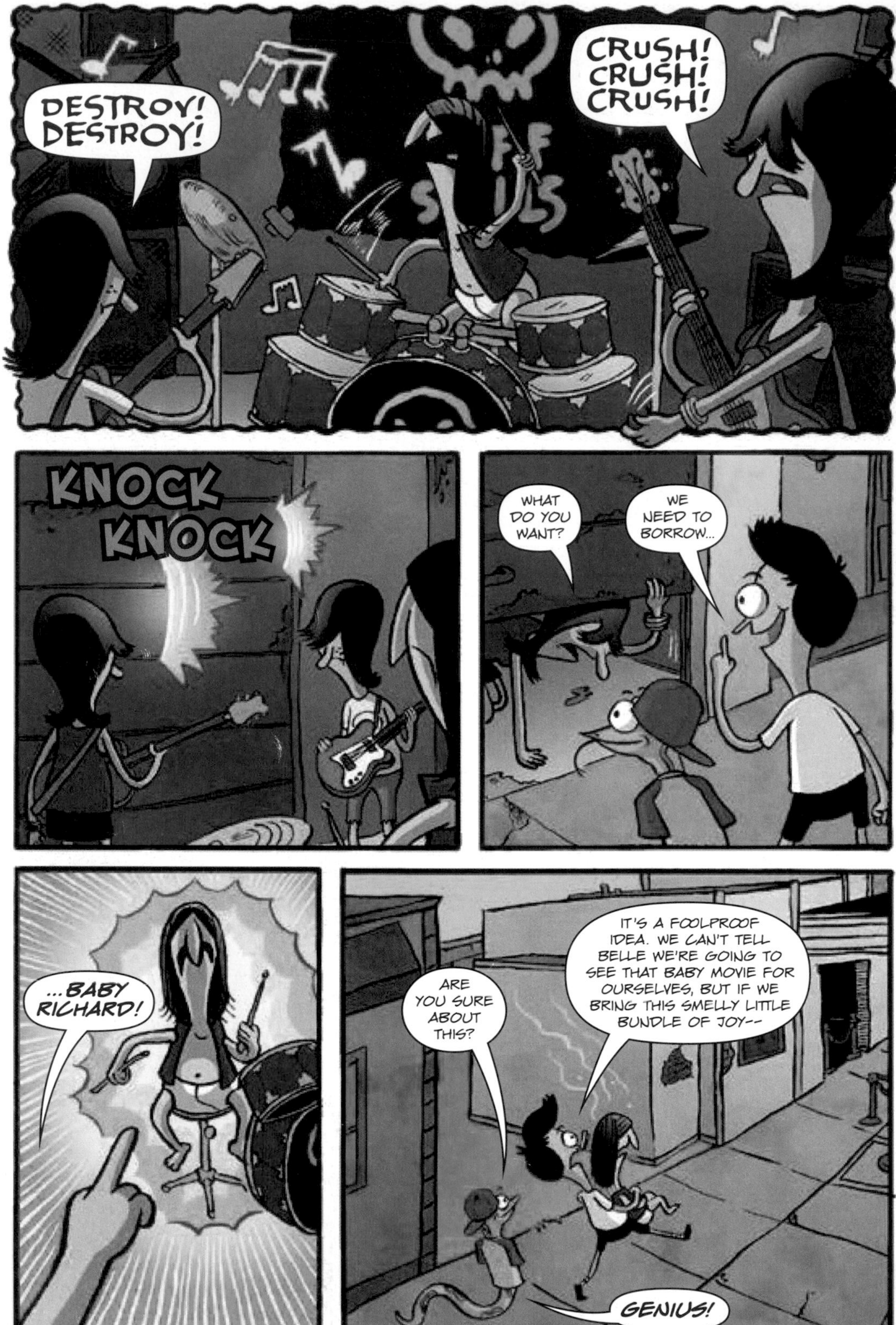
DESTROY! DESTROY!
CRUSH! CRUSH! CRUSH!
KNOCK KNOCK
WHAT DO YOU WANT?
WE NEED TO BORROW...
...BABY RICHARD!
IT'S A FOOLPROOF IDEA. WE CAN'T TELL BELLE WE'RE GOING TO SEE THAT BABY MOVIE FOR OURSELVES, BUT IF WE BRING THIS SMELLY LITTLE BUNDLE OF JOY--
ARE YOU SURE ABOUT THIS?
GENIUS!

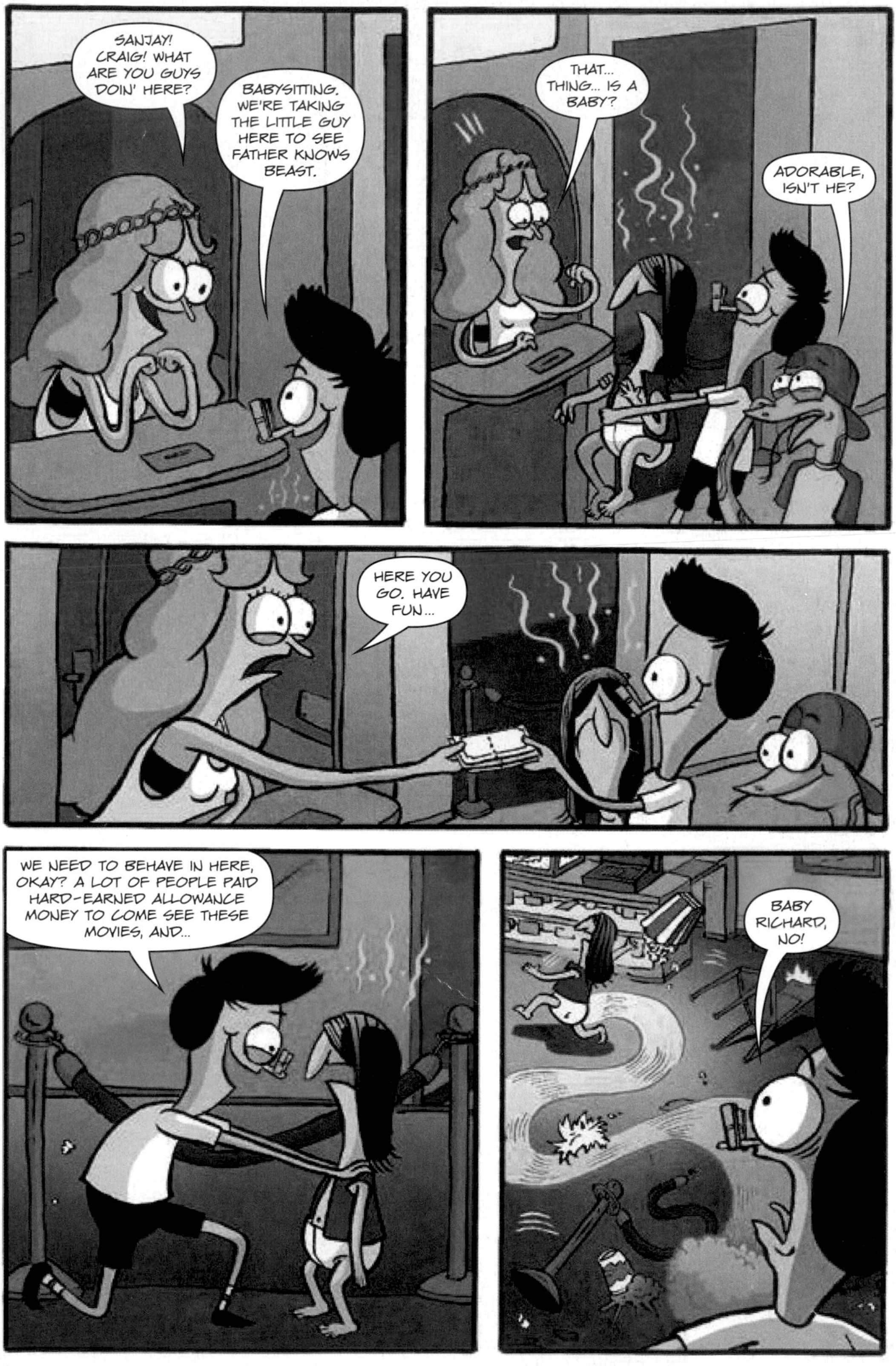
SANJAY! CRAIG! WHAT ARE YOU GUYS DOIN' HERE?
BABYSITTING. WE'RE TAKING THE LITTLE GUY HERE TO SEE FATHER KNOWS BEAST.
THAT... THING... IS A BABY?
ADORABLE, ISN'T HE?
HERE YOU GO. HAVE FUN...
WE NEED TO BEHAVE IN HERE, OKAY? A LOT OF PEOPLE PAID HARD-EARNED ALLOWANCE MONEY TO COME SEE THESE MOVIES, AND...
BABY RICHARD, NO!

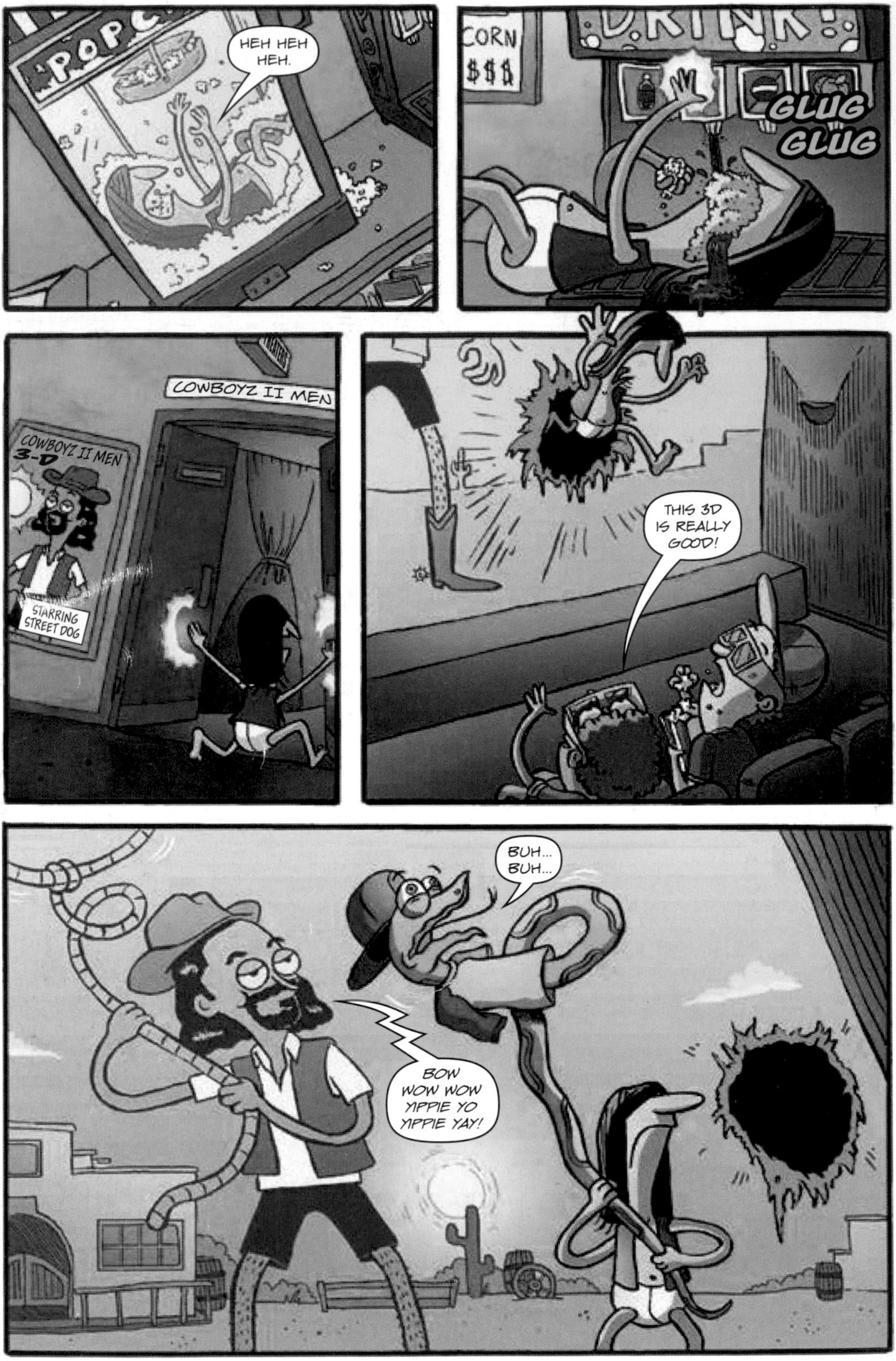
HEH HEH HEH.
CORN $$$
DRINK!
GLUG GLUG
COWBOYZ II MEN
COWBOYZ II MEN 3-D
STARRING STREET DOG
THIS 3D IS REALLY GOOD!
BUH... BUH...
BOW WOW WOW YIPPIE YO YIPPIE YAY!

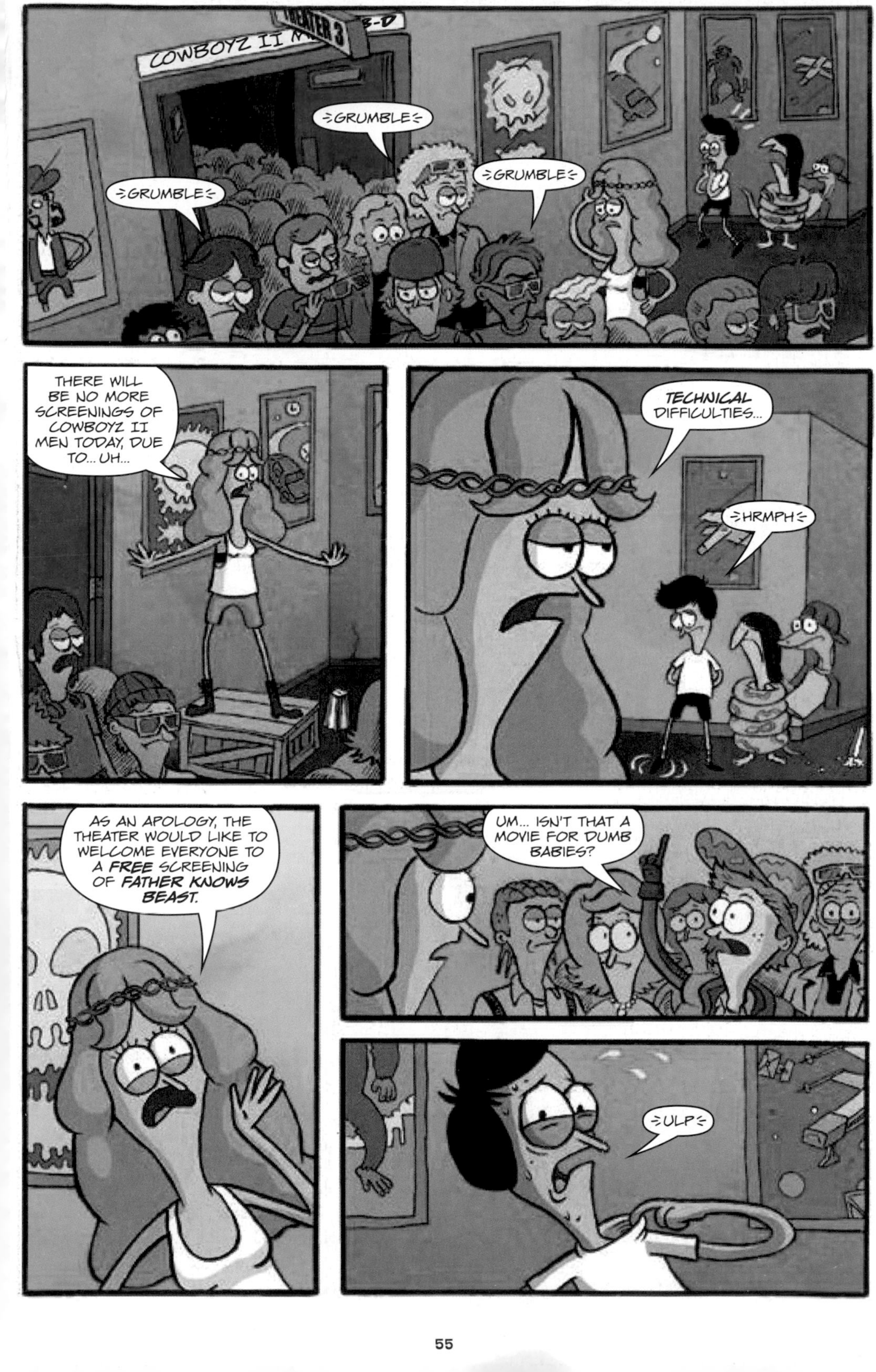
COWBOYZ II M
THEATER 3
GRUMBLE
GRUMBLE
GRUMBLE
THERE WILL BE NO MORE SCREENINGS OF COWBOYZ II MEN TODAY, DUE TO... UH...
TECHNICAL DIFFICULTIES...
HRMPH
AS AN APOLOGY, THE THEATER WOULD LIKE TO WELCOME EVERYONE TO A FREE SCREENING OF FATHER KNOWS BEAST.
UM... ISN'T THAT A MOVIE FOR DUMB BABIES?
ULP

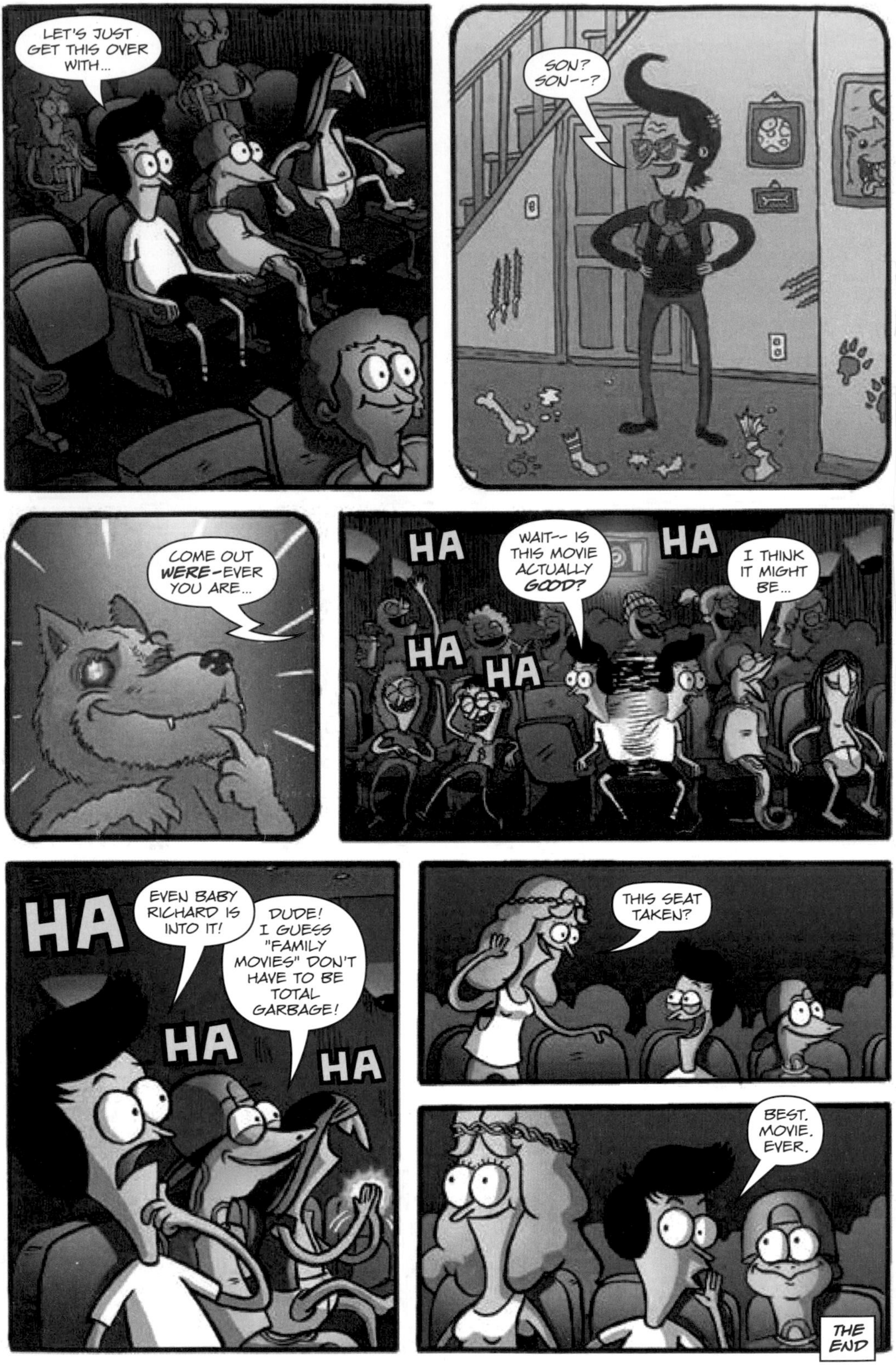
LET'S JUST GET THIS OVER WITH...
SON? SON--?
COME OUT WERE-EVER YOU ARE...
HA
WAIT-- IS THIS MOVIE ACTUALLY GOOD?
HA
I THINK IT MIGHT BE...
HA
HA
HA
EVEN BABY RICHARD IS INTO IT!
DUDE! I GUESS "FAMILY MOVIES" DON'T HAVE TO BE TOTAL GARBAGE!
HA
HA
THIS SEAT TAKEN?
BEST. MOVIE. EVER.
THE END